Tales told Again

also by Walter de la Mare

COLLECTED RHYMES AND VERSES
PEACOCK PIE (Faber Fanfares)
STORIES FROM THE BIBLE

Tales told Again

by

WALTER DE LA MARE

illustrated by

ALAN HOWARD

FABER
FANFARES

First published in 1927
by Basil Blackwell Limited
under the title of 'Told Again'
First published in 1959
by Faber and Faber Limited
3 Queen Square London WC1
First published in Fanfares edition 1980
Printed in Great Britain by
Jarrold and Sons Ltd, Norwich
All rights reserved

CONDITIONS OF SALE

British Library Cataloguing in Publication Data

de la Mare, Walter
Tales told again. – (Faber fanfares).
I. Title II. Howard, Alan, *b. 1922*
823'.9'1J   PZ7.D3724

ISBN 0–571–18013–2

Contents

The Hare and the Hedgehog

Early one Sunday morning, when the cowslips or paigles were showing their first honey-sweet buds in the meadows and the broom was in bloom, a hedgehog came to his little door to look out at the weather. He stood with arms a-kimbo, whistling a tune to himself—a tune no better and no worse than the tunes hedgehogs usually whistle to themselves on fine Sunday mornings. And as he whistled, the notion came into his head that, before turning in and while his wife was washing the children, he might take a little walk into the fields and see how his young nettles were getting on. For there was a tasty beetle lived among the nettles; and no nettles —no beetles.

Off he went, taking his own little private path into the field. And as he came stepping along around a bush of blackthorn, its blossoming now over and its leaves showing green, he met a hare; and the hare had come out to look at his spring cabbages.

The hedgehog smiled and bade him a polite "Good-morning". But the hare, who felt himself a particularly fine sleek gentleman in this Sunday sunshine, merely sneered at his greeting.

"And how is it," he said, "*you* happen to be out so early?"

The Hare and the Hedgehog

"I am taking a walk, sir," said the hedgehog.

"A walk!" sniffed the hare. "I should have thought you might use those bandy little legs of yours to far better purpose."

This angered the hedgehog, for as his legs were crooked by nature, he couldn't bear to have bad made worse by any talk about them.

"You seem to suppose, sir," he said, bristling all over, "that you can do more with your legs than I can with mine."

"Well, perhaps," said the hare, airily.

"See here, then," said the hedgehog, his beady eyes fixed on the hare, "I say you *can't*. Start fair, and I'd beat you nowt to ninepence. Ay, every time."

"A race, my dear Master Hedgehog!" said the hare, laying back his whiskers. "You must be beside yourself. It's *childish*. But still, what will you wager?"

"I'll lay a Golden Guinea to a Bottle of Brandy," said the hedgehog.

"Done!" said the hare. "Shake hands on it, and we'll start at once."

"Ay, but not quite so fast," said the hedgehog. "I have had no breakfast yet. But if you will be here in half an hour's time, so will I."

The hare agreed, and at once took a little frisky practice along the dewy green border of the field, while the hedgehog went shuffling home.

"He thinks a mighty deal of himself," thought the hedgehog on his way. "But we shall see what we *shall* see." When he reached home he bustled in and looking solemnly at his wife said:

"My dear, I have need of you. In all haste. Leave everything and follow me at once into the fields."

"Why, what's going on?" says she.

The Hare and the Hedgehog

"Why," said her husband, "I have bet the hare a guinea to a Bottle of Brandy that I'll beat him in a race, and you must come and see it."

"Heavens! husband," Mrs. Hedgehog cried, "are you daft? Are you gone crazy? You! Run a race with a hare!"

"Hold your tongue, woman," said the hedgehog. "There are things simple brains cannot understand. Leave all this fussing and titivating. The children can dry themselves; and you come along at once with me." So they went together.

"Now," said the hedgehog, when they reached the ploughed field beyond the field which was sprouting with young green wheat, "listen to me, my dear. This is where the race is going to be. The hare is over there at the other end of the field. I am going to arrange that he shall start in that deep furrow, and I shall start in this. But as soon as I have scrambled along a few inches and he

11

can't see me, I shall turn back. And what *you*, my dear, must do is this: When he comes out of his furrow *there*, you must be sitting puffing like a porpoise *here*. And when you see him, you will say, 'Ahah! so you've come at last?' Do you follow me, my dear?" At first Mrs. Hedgehog was a little nervous, but she smiled at her husband's cunning, and gladly agreed to do what he said.

The hedgehog then went back to where he had promised to meet the hare, and he said, "Here I am, you see; and very much the better, sir, for a good breakfast."

"How shall we run," simpered the hare scornfully, "down or over; sideways, longways; three legs or altogether? It's all one to me."

"Well, to be honest with you," said the hedgehog, "let me say this. I have now and then watched you taking a gambol and disporting yourself with your friends in the evening, and a pretty runner you are. But you never keep straight. You all go round and round, and round and round, scampering now this way, now that and chasing one another's scuts as if you were crazy. And as often as not you run uphill! But you can't run *races* like that. You must keep straight; you must begin in one place, go steadily on, and end in another."

"I could have told you that," said the hare angrily.

"Very well then," said the hedgehog. "You shall keep to that furrow, and I'll keep to this."

And the hare, being a good deal quicker on his feet than he was in his wits, agreed.

"*One, Two! Three!—and AWAY!*" he shouted, and off he went like a little whirlwind up the field. But the hedgehog, after scuttling along a few paces, turned back and stayed quietly where he was.

When the hare came out of his furrow at the upper end of the field, the hedgehog's wife sat panting there as if she would never be able to recover her breath, and at sight of him she sighed out, "Ahah! sir, so you've come at last?"

The hare was utterly shocked. His ears trembled. His eyes bulged in his head. "You've run it! You've run it!" he cried in astonishment. For she being so exactly like her husband, he never for a moment doubted that her husband she actually was.

"Ay," said she, "but I was afraid you had gone lame."

"Lame!" said the hare, "lame! But there, what's one furrow? 'Every time' was what you said. We'll try again."

Away once more he went, and he had never run faster. Yet when he came out of his furrow at the bottom of the field, there was the hedgehog! And the hedgehog laughed, and said: "Ahah! So here you are again! At last!" At this the hare could hardly speak for rage.

"Not enough! not enough!" he said. "Three for luck! Again, again!"

"As often as you please, my dear friend," said the hedgehog. "It's the long run that really counts."

Again, and again, and yet again the hare raced up and down the long furrow of the field, and every time he reached the top, and every time he reached the bottom, there was the hedgehog, as he thought, with his mocking, "Ahah! So here you are again! At last!"

But at length the hare could run no more. He lay panting and speechless; he was dead beat. Stretched out there, limp on the grass, his fur bedraggled, his eyes dim, his legs quaking, it looked as if he might fetch his last breath at any moment.

So Mrs. Hedgehog went off to the hare's house to fetch the Bottle of Brandy; and, if it had not been the best brandy, the hare might never have run again.

The Hare and the Hedgehog

News of the contest spread far and wide. From that day to this, never has there been a race to compare with it. And lucky it was for the hedgehog he had the good sense to marry a wife like himself, and not a weasel, or a wombat, or a whale!

The Four Brothers

In the days of long ago, there was a farmer who had four sons. His was not a big farm; he had only a small flock of sheep, a few cows, and not much plough or meadow land. But he was well content. His sons had always been with him, either on his own farm or near-about, and he had grown to love them more and more. Never man had better sons than he had.

For this reason he grew ill at ease at the thought of what they were giving up for his sake; and at last one day he called them together and said to them: "There will be little left, when I am gone, to divide up amongst four. Journey off, then, my dear sons, into the great world; seek your fortunes, and see what you can do for yourselves. Find each of you as honest and profitable a trade as he can; come back to me in four years' time, and we shall see how you have all prospered. And God's blessing go with you!"

So his four sons cut themselves cudgels out of the hedge, made up their bundles, and off they went. After waving their father goodbye at the gate, they trudged along the high-road together till they came to cross-roads, where four ways met. Here they parted one from another, since on any road there is more room for one than for four. Then off each went again, whistling into the morning.

After he had gone a few miles, the first and eldest of them met a stranger who asked him where he was bound for. "By the looks of you," he said, "you might be in sight of the Spice Islands." He told him he was off to try his luck in the world.

"Well," said the stranger, "come along with me, and I will teach you to be nimble with your fingers. Nimble of fingers is nimble of wits. And I'll warrant when I've done with you, you'll be able to snipple-snupple away any mortal thing you have an eye to, and nobody so much as guess it's gone."

"Not me," said the other. "That's thieving. Old Master Take-What-He-Wanted was hanged on a gallows. And there, for all I care, he hangs still."

"Ay," said the old man, "that he were. But that old Master Take-What-He-Wanted you are talking of was a villainous rogue and a rascal. But supposing you're only after borrowing its lamp from a glow-worm, or a loaf of bread from a busy bee, what then? Follow along now; you shall see!"

So off they went together. And very well they did.

The second son had not gone far when he chanced on an old man sitting under a flowering bush and eating bread and cheese and an onion with a jack-knife. The old man said to him, "Good-morning, my friend. What makes you so happy?"

He said, "I am off to seek my fortune."

"Ah," said the old man, "then come along with me; for one's fortune is with the stars, and I am an astronomer, and a star-gazer." In a bag beside him, this old pilgrim showed the young man a set of glasses for spying out the stars, glasses that had come from Arabia and those parts. After looking through the glasses, the young man needed no persuasion and went along with him. And very well they did.

The third brother, having turned off into the greenwood, soon met a jolly huntsman with a horn and a quiver full of arrows on his shoulder. The huntsman liked the fine fresh look of the lad. He promised to teach him his ancient art and skill with the bow; so they went along together. And very well they did.

The youngest brother tramped on many a mile before he met anybody, and he was resting under a tree listening to the birds and enjoying a morsel of food out of his bundle, when a tailor came along, with crooked legs and one eye. And the tailor said to him, "Plenty to do, but nothing doing!"

The boy laughed, and said, "I have been walking all morning, having just left my dear old father for the first time. Now I am resting a moment, for I am off into the world to get my living and to see if I can bring him back something worth having; and if I don't, then may my fingers grow thumbs!"

And the tailor, prettily taken by his way of speaking, said, "If you are wishful to learn a craft, young man, come along with me." So off they went together. And very well they did.

Now, after four years to the very day, the four brothers met again at the cross-roads and returned to their father. A pleasant meeting it was. For though their old father was getting on in years, he had worked on alone at the farm with a good heart, feeling sure that his sons were doing well in the world and making their way. That night when they were all, as in old times, sitting together at supper—two of his sons on either side of him, and himself in the middle—he said to them: "Now, good sons all, tell me your adventures, and what you've been doing these long years past. And I promise you it will be well worth hearing."

The four brothers looked at one another, and the eldest said:

"Ay, so we will, father, if you'll wait till to-morrow. Then we will do whatever you ask us, to show we have learned our trades and not been idle. Think over to-night what you'd like us to do in the morning, and we'll all be ready."

The old man's one fear that night as he lay in bed thinking of the morrow was lest he might give his sons too hard a thing to do. But before he could think of anything that seemed not too hard yet not too easy, he fell asleep.

The next morning, after the five of them had gobbled up their breakfast, they went out into the fields together. Then the old man said:

"Up in the branches of that tree, my sons, is a chaffinch's nest, and there the little hen is sitting. Now could any one of you tell me how many eggs she has under her?" For he thought the youngest would climb into the tree, scare off the bird, and count them.

But nothing so simple as that. "Why, yes, father," said the second son, and taking out of his pocket a certain optic glass his master had given him as a parting present, he put it to his best eye, looked up, squinnied through it, and said, "Five".

At this the old man was exceedingly pleased, for he knew he told him the truth.

"Now," says he, "could one of you *get* those eggs for me, and maybe without alarming the mother-bird over-much? Eh? What about that?"

There and then the eldest son, who had been taught by

his master every trick there is for nimble fingers, shinned up into the tree, and dealt with the little bird so gently that he took all her five eggs into the hollow of his hand without disturbing even the littlest and downiest of her feathers in the nest.

The old man marvelled and said, "Better and better! But now, see here," he went on, gently laying the five eggs on a flat patch of mossy turf, and turning to the son who had gone off with the huntsman—"now, shoot me all these, my son, with one arrow. My faith, 'twould be a master stroke!"

His son went off a full fifty paces, and drawing the little black bow made of sinew (which his master had bought from the Tartars), with a tiny twang of its string he loosed a needle-sharp arrow that, one after the other, pierced all five eggs as neatly as a squirrel cracks nuts.

"Ha, ha!" cried the old man, almost dumbfounded, and prouder than ever of them all, then turned to his youngest son. "Ay, and can *you*, my son, put them together again?" But this he meant only in jest.

With that, the youngest son sat down at the foot of the tree, and there and then, and they all watching, with the needle and thread which had once been his master's he sewed the shells together so deftly that even with his second son's magic glass his old father could scarcely see the stitches. This being done, the eggs were put back into the nest again, and the mother-bird sat out her time. Moreover, the only thing strange in her five nestlings when they were all safely hatched out of their shells was that each had a fine crimson thread of silk neatly stitched round its neck—which made her as vain and proud of her brood as the old father was of his four sons.

"Now stay with me for a time," he entreated them. "There is plenty to eat and drink, and there are a few little odd jobs you might do for me while you are with me. Never man had better sons, and a joy it is beyond words to have you all safely home again."

So they said they would stay with their old father as long as he wished.

However, they had scarcely been a week at home when news came that a Dragon which had been prowling near one of the King's castles that was built at the edge of a vast fen, or bogland, had carried off the Princess, his only daughter. The whole realm was in grief and dread at this news, and the King in despair had decreed that any-one who should discover the Dragon and bring back the Princess should have her for wife. After pondering this news awhile the old farmer said to his sons:

"Now, my lads, here's a chance indeed. Not that I'm saying it's good for a man, as I think, to marry anybody he has no mind to. But to save any manner of human creature from a cruel foul Dragon—who wouldn't have a try?"

So the four brothers set out at once to the Castle, and were taken before the King. They asked the King where the Dragon was. And the King groaned, "Who knows?"

So the Star-gazer put up his spy-glass to his eye, and peered long through its tube—north, east, south, then west. And he said at last, "*I* see him, sire, a full day's sailingaway. He is coiled up grisly on a rock with his wings folded, at least a league to sea, and his hooked great clanking tail curled round him. Ay, and I see the Princess too, no bigger than my little finger in size, beside him. She's been crying, by the looks of her. And the Dragon is keeping mighty sly guard over her, for one of his eyes is an inch ajar."

The King greatly wondered, and sent word to the Queen, who was in a chamber apart; and he gave the four brothers a ship, and they sailed away in the King's ship until they neared the island and the rock. In great caution they then took in sail, drifting slowly in. When they were come near and in green water under the rock, they saw that the Princess was now asleep, worn out with grief and despair, and that her head lay so close to the Dragon that her hair was spread out like yellow silk upon its horny scales.

"Shoot I dare not," said the huntsman, "for, by Nimrod, I might pierce the heart of the Princess."

So first the nimble-fingered brother swam ashore, and creeping up behind the Dragon, stole and withdrew the Princess away with such ease and cunning that the monster thought only a gentle breeze had wafted upon its coils with its wings. Stealthy as a seal he slipped into the sea again and swam back to the ship, the Princess lying cradled in the water nearby him, for, though she could not swim herself, she rode almost as light on the water as a sea-bird. Then the four brothers hoisted sail and with all haste sailed away.

But the ship had hardly sailed a league and a league when the Dragon, turning softly in his drowsiness, became aware that a fragrance had gone out of the morning. And when he found that his captive was lost to him he raised his head with so lamentable a cry the very rocks

resounded beneath the screaming of the sea-birds; then writhing his neck this way and that, he descried the white sails of the ship on the horizon like a bubble in the air. Whereupon he spread his vast, bat-like wings and, soaring into the heavens, pursued the ship across the sea.

The four brothers heard from afar the dreadful clanging of his scales, but waited till he was near at hand. When at last he was circling overhead, his hooked and horny wings darkening the very light of the sun, the huntsman, with one mighty twang of his bow-string, let fly an arrow, and the arrow sped clean through the Dragon from tip of snout to utmost barb of tail, and he fell like a millstone. So close, however, in his flight had he approached the ship, that his huge carcase crashed flat upon it in the sea and shattered it to pieces.

But by marvellous good fortune the Dragon fell on that half of the ship which is between the bowsprit and mainmast, so that neither the Princess nor the four brothers came to any harm (for they were in the parts abaft the mainmast), except that one and all were flung helter-skelter into the sea. There they would certainly have drowned but for the tailor son, who at once straddled a baulk of timber, and, drawing in every plank within reach as it came floating by, speedily stitched up a raft with his magic needle. Soon all the other three brothers had clambered up out of the sea on to the raft, and having lifted the Princess as gently as might be after them, they came at last safely ashore.

There, sitting on the sunny shingle of the beach, they dried their clothes in the sun, and the Princess sleeked her hair, and when she had refreshed herself with a morsel of honeycomb which the Star-gazer found in the heart of a hollow tree, the four brothers led her safely back to the Palace; and great were the rejoicings.

The King, having listened to their story, marvelled, and bade that a great feast should be prepared. A little before the hour fixed for this feast, he sent for these brothers, and they stood beside his chair.

"Now, which of you," he said, "is to have the Princess to wife? For each did wondrous well: the spying out, the stealing away, the death-wound, and the rafting. Her life is yours, but she cannot be cut into quarters," and he smiled at them all. "Still, a King is as good as his word; and no man can do better. Do you decide."

Then the four brothers withdrew a little and talked together in a corner of the great hall. Then they came back to the King, and the eldest thanked the King for them all, and said:

"We are, Liege, sons of one dear father, who is a farmer.

If of your graciousness your Majesty would see that he is never in want, and that he prospers howsoever long he lives, and even though he live to be an old, old man and can work no more, we shall be your happy and contented subjects to the end of our days. You see, we might die, your Majesty, and then our poor old father would have to live alone with none to help him."

The King stroked his beard and smiled on them.

"Besides, your Majesty," he went on, "never was Princess more beautiful than she we have brought back in safety, but a dragon dead is dead for ever, and no pretty maid we ever heard of, high or low, but wished to choose a husband for herself, whatever dragons there might be to prevent her."

At this the King laughed aloud, and the Queen bade the four brothers come and sit on either side of her at the banquet, two by two, and the Princess kissed each of them on the cheek. Then they showed their marvels and their skill; and there was music and delight until the stars in the heavens showed it to be two in the morning.

Next day the four brothers set out together for home, with twelve fen horses, which have long manes and tails and are of a rusty red, and each of these horses was laden with two sacks one on either side, and each sack was bulging full of gifts for the four brothers and for their old father. And a pleasant journey home that was.

The Musicians

Once upon a time, there was a poor old ass. After toiling for eighteen years carrying meal for his master, who was a miller, he was now nothing much better than a bag of bones. And one cold, frosty night, as he was standing close up beside the mills to get a little warmth from the wall behind which was the kitchen fire, he heard the miller say to his wife:

"The old ass must go, my love. He's been a good servant, but now he's long past his prime. Why, he doesn't even earn his keep. He's not worth a ha'penny more than his skin."

"If skin it is," said his wife, "then skin it must be. We'll make an end of him to-morrow."

The old ass shivered as he heard these words; his old knobble knees shook under him; but he didn't wait for morning. Not he. He set out at once, thinking to himself: "Whatever happens to me now, it can't be worse than a skinning." And because it chanced to be the first road he came to after leaving the mill, he chose the road that leads to Bremen.

An hour or two after daybreak, he came on his journey to an ancient stone Cross, green with moss and grey with lichen; and stretched out beneath it lay an old hound. This hound told the ass that he had run away from his master, who was a huntsman.

"After serving him all my life long I heard him say only two days ago that my scent and wind were gone, that I wasn't worth a beef-bone, and that all I was good for was to make cat's-meat of me."

"Well," said the donkey, "to tell you the truth, sir, I am in much the same case myself. But, as you see, I can still bray a little; and you, I am sure, can raise an honest howl if need be. Let us, then, journey on to Bremen together—the two of us—and join the town band. I have heard they are fine musicians, and I am sure we shall be welcome."

So they went on together. But they had not gone more than a mile or two—and pretty slow they were at it—when what should they see but an old grey tabby cat, sitting up with her toes tucked in on an orchard wall in the sun, and with a face as long as three rainy days in December.

"A very good-morning to you, madam," said the ass. "You are not looking so bright as might be."

"Bright!" said the cat. "Nor would you be. The very instant my mistress can catch me, she's going to drown me. And why?—because I am old and worn out—worn out with mousing for her and singing under her window. Night after night I have amused her with my purring when she wanted company, played games with her with her knitting, and shown her every affection. But no pity! no mercy! Ay, my friends, it's a string and a stone for me to-morrow; and I'm basking in this warm sunshine while I can."

"They are all of them like that," said the old hound.

"Most; but not all," said the ass. "Now, pray listen to me, madam. My friend, here, and I have a plan. We are off to Bremen to join the town band. I'll be bound you can still pipe up a stave or two when a full moon's up aloft. There are, I am told, very good—or, at least, very fair—musicians in Bremen. Come with us, then, and we will all three go together. I doubt if the good people of Bremen have ever had such a chance before."

So these three old creatures journeyed on together, and pretty slowly the miles went by, for it was a long way to trudge. Indeed, without knowing it, they had lost themselves for some time past, when they came to a tumbledown shed near a duck-pond. And there, perched on the roof of the shed, was an old barn-door cock. This old cock, all ruffled and woebegone, looked even more doleful than the cat. The ass politely asked him the way to Bremen, and the cock told them that they were at least five miles out of it.

"As for me," he said, "the only way *I* want is to a better world. My master, the Farmer yonder, says I'm no use to him now, though I have kept watch over his hens and his eggs ever since my spurs began to sprout. Not a midnight has passed, summer or winter, but I've warned him it would soon be time for him to get up. And who dares venture into the farmyard while *I* guard his dunghill! But no: all forgotten! No mercy! He's going to wring my neck to-morrow. And my poor old bones are not even marrowy enough to be worth broiling for his supper!"

"They are all like that," said the hound.

"Most; but not all," said the ass. "And I'll wager, Master Chanticleer, that you can still yell *cockadoodle* when dawn's in the East."

"Why, so!" said the cock, at once preening himself a little out of his dumps. And softly, lest the Farmer should hear him, he flapped his sheeny wings and crowed "*Cockadoodle-oo-do!*"

The ass said: "Bravo, friend! A true note; a shrill

27

high mellow note; an excellent note. Come along with *us*, sir! We are all off to Bremen to join the town band. One's one. Two's two. Three's three. But four's a Quartette!"

So off they went together. But being all of them old, feeble, and in strange parts, they once more lost their way. Worse, it was now pitch-dark, and there was no shelter to be seen. So, after they had talked things over, the old cock flew up into a fir tree that stood nearby, and after a little while he called down to them and said: "With my round eye I see the twinkling of a light."

So on they went once more, but with great caution, and presently came to a fine stone house beside a stream. And a marvellous bright light was shining in its lower windows.

They whispered together in the dark, and at last the old cat crept off, and soft as a shadow leapt up clean on to the window-sill and looked in through the glass. When she came back, she told her friends that there was a great feast going on within—a blazing fire and hosts of candles, and a table laden with food—pies, and game, and wines, and sweetmeats.

"I could scarcely see out of my eyes for the glare," she said. "Ay, and they must be robbers, for the tables and chairs are piled up with gold and silver dishes and goblets, and there is a huge burst bag of money on the floor. Never have I seen such a sight!"

"Well," said the ass, "I must confess, friends, *I* could munch up a loaf of fine white bread. Ay, and say grace after it."

The old hound's mouth watered as he thought of chicken bones; and Grimalkin's whiskers twitched with rapture at the memory not only of the rich soup and cream she had seen on the table, but, above all, a dish of boned, broiled fish.

Then the cock said: "Let's give them a stave of our music, my friends. Perhaps, robbers though they be, and though they may all live to be hanged, they might spare us a bite of supper."

So all four of them, in utter silence, crept up as close as might be beneath the window. Then the old hound leapt up and sat on the donkey's back; the cat leapt up and sat on the hound's back; and last, the cock flew up and perched on the cat's back, so that the sound of their voices when they gave vent together should fall as one on the ears of the robbers, and not part by part.

Then, at a signal, they all burst into song. In the dead silence of night the sudden noise and clamour of their voices was like the yelling of fourscore demons out of a pit. At sound of it the robbers leapt from their chairs in terror, and, supposing a whole regiment at least of the King's soldiers were after them, made such haste to be gone that they overturned the lights, and, except for the blazing of the fire, left the whole house in darkness.

So our four companions went in, sat down merrily together at the table and feasted as if they were never going to taste bite or sup again. But first the ass drew the curtains over the window. And when they had finished their supper—which was not too soon—these old minstrels, who were now fast friends indeed, bade each other good night.

The ass made himself snug and cosy on some bundles of straw in the yard; the hound lay down behind the door; the cat curled herself up head to tail in the warm ashes; and the cock flew up on to the curtain rod—there to roost till morning. Soon, in good comfort after the feast they had shared, they were all four of them fast asleep.

About midnight, the robbers, having at last taken

courage again, crept back to the house to get their plunder, and seeing that no light now shone in the windows, and that all within was still as the grave, the Captain of the robbers bade one of his men make his way into the house and see exactly what had befallen and what he could find.

Quaking with terror, the robber crept softly in at the window. It was warm within, but pitch-dark; and supposing that the bright green eyes of the cat, as she glared up at him, were coals smouldering in the fire, he stooped down to light a candle. But puss thought this a very poor joke, and squealing with fury, spitting and scratching and claws on end, leapt straight up into his face. A fine mauling he got.

Half-scared out of his wits, the robber ran to the door and, stumbling over the hound, fell headlong, whereupon the hound sprang up, and with the few teeth left in his head bit clean through his leg. The robber rushed across the yard into the straw, and so fell pell-mell over the ass, who gave him in return a mighty smart kick with his hoof. At this the cock on the curtain rod, who had been at once awakened by the din, flew down from his roosting-place and yelled after him as he had never yelled before.

So the robber fled back to his Captain and cried, "Away, Captain, away! There's a witch in the house! With eyes like saucers and talons like hooks! She spat at me and scravelled at me with her claws. By the door was an assassin with a knife, who stabbed me in the leg; and in the yard is a foul, four-handed monster that beat me with a club. Then a demon out of the clouds pursued me, yelling, 'Death to the Robbers! Death to the Robbers!' and I have but just escaped with my life."

This band of rascals never ventured near *that* house

again. And it proved so snug and comfortable that the four friends decided not to go on to Bremen yet awhile, but, living there at ease, to practise their singing and their minstrelsy first. Morning and evening they raise their voices together, and a mighty fine music they make. And if ever you should happen to go that way, and should come to a fine stone house in a forest beside a stream, maybe you will hear sweet strains at the window as they sing their quartette.

Dick Whittington

————————)0⊕0(‹————————

In days of old, there was a boy named Dick who was an orphan. His father and mother had died when he was young; so he was alone in the world; and the only living he could get was by keeping pigs in the forest. He had little to eat, rags to wear, and watched his pigs with envy as they nuzzled and grunted after their beech-mast and acorns, and grew fat and hearty. And few live things are heartier than a clean, comely pig. The only friend Dick had in the world was his cat.

Now this cat of Dick's was a fine, sleek, black cat, very wary on its feet, and with bright green eyes. It never miaowed and seldom purred. But it was exceedingly fond of its master, ragged Dick, and—almost as if to show him its affection—would sometimes bring him a wild bird out of the bushes, and, laying it at his feet, look up through its green eyes into his face, as if to say, "Share a bite with me, master."

Then Dick would laugh at his cat, and scratch its head. He loved its company.

One day in his ramblings with his pigs through the forest, Dick met a charcoal-burner, who gave him a sip out of his bottle. Dick stayed to talk, and as they sat together by his fire the charcoal-burner told him of his travels and adventures in all parts of the country and in other countries too. And Dick asked him about London.

"It's a fine city," said the charcoal-burner, "full of rich men and fine ladies and great houses, and a fine wide river with boats and bridges, and shops blazing like Old Moses, and booths, and stalls laid out with pigs' trotters and mutton-pies, and streets paved with gold. Oh, it's a fine city!"

"And what would a boy like me find to do there?" said Dick Whittington, for that was his full name.

"Why," says the charcoal-burner, stirring up the fire with his foot, "make his fortune." And he laughed.

Dick looked at the charcoal-burner in the blaze of the fire, and when he had gone back to his pigs, he began thinking about what had been told him. He built a London in his mind. He could all but smell those mutton-pies. And half-believing the charcoal-burner's stories, he vowed he would take the road next morning and tramp off to London; and when once Dick had decided on anything he did it.

So early next morning he left his pigs in the forest, for he was afraid to go back to his master, and with his cat under his jacket, set off on his way to London. It chanced, when he reached there, that the sun was shining clear and low in the West, so that the streets with their churches and mansions looked dazzling as gold, and there was a concourse of rich men in the streets walking about or riding on horseback, and fine shops; and he came to the river, which was in flood, and there were carts and ped-lars. At night, too, he saw the Lord Mayor go by—with link-boys carrying torches—in his great gilded coach, and footmen like fat porpoises.

But next day it was different. He came to filthy alleys and courts where thieves and beggars lived, and half-starved children played in the streets. And, try as he might, Dick couldn't get work. Nobody would look at him because of his rags. They thought him a sneak-thief or pickpocket. The women in the houses where he knocked slammed the door in his face. The curs in the streets snapped at his heels because of his cat, and Puss was soon in a worse temper than it had ever been in before.

But night came down, the noise of the streets ebbed away, the lights went out in the windows, and after a short nap Dick's cat stole off and had a hearty meal off a slab of fish it managed to steal off a fishmonger's stall. It then caught a black rat and brought it next morning to Dick as he lay asleep on the doorstep of an empty shop.

Now it chanced that morning that a certain merchant (as he went about his business) passed by the place where Dick lay, and he saw Dick (bedraggled with dirt, bony and ragged) huddled asleep there on the doorstep, with his cat curled up beside him. There, too, the black rat lay, dead upon the step. The merchant smiled to himself at sight of the cat and the rat, then stooped and looked closer into the boy's face. And as Dick lay asleep his face, meagre and grimy though it was, looked gentle and honest, and not sharp or cunning. The merchant liked the looks of the lad.

He shook him gently by the shoulder, and having there and then heard Dick's story, he asked him, How would it be if he gave Dick work to do in his own warehouse? "A chance, my lad," said he, "to prove what you're made of."

At this, tears of joy came into Dick's eyes, for he was deadly footsore and hungry. But the first thing he said was, "Please, sir, if I come may I bring my cat?"

"Why," said the merchant heartily, "Puss will be as welcome as you are, for my warehouse is packed with grain and oil and flour and bacon, so there are rats by the hundred and mice by the ten thousand. It will be a fine brisk living for your cat, and good for my merchandise."

The cat looked up at the merchant, and licked its chops.

For a time Dick was happy enough at his work. But the huge warehouse at night was dark and solitary—nothing to be heard but squeaks and scamperings and creakings, and the chuckle and gentle drumming of the tide on the stones and timbers of the walls of the warehouse, for it was built out upon its wharf in the river—and Dick began after some months to be restless and ill at ease. At last, one night in spring, he could bear himself no longer. He clean forgot the promise he had made to his master to work with him for seven years. Worse still, he forgot the merchant's kindness, for, if it had not been for that, Dick might long ago have starved in the streets. It seemed to him that if he stayed in the warehouse a moment longer he would be suffocated. So, with his cat under his arm, he crept out of the warehouse into the moonlight, and at first, as if frightened at the sound of his own footsteps, ran away as fast as he could, then fell into a walk, and at last came to the hill of Highgate.

When morning broke, he found himself sitting in the dew-laden grass under a hedge on this hill, a few miles out of London, but not so far that he could not hear her bells ringing. He listened to the sound of the bells stealing over the fields, for then the country was close to the city, with its woods and waters; and the bells as they rang seemed to be taking words in their voices, and saying:

> *"Turn–a–gain–Whit–ting–ton!*
> *Come–back–Dick–Whit–ting–ton!*
> *Lord–Mayor–of–London–town!"*

And as Dick listened to the bells, fancying these words, he thought of his master, and his cat was cleaning its face with its paw. Four and forty times Puss passed its paw over the ear on that side of its face which was towards London. Dick counted, still listening to the bells. When, for the last time, having licked its paw, it smoothed it gently again over the same ear, it paused in its washing and looked up at its young master. It seemed to be listening too, while yet once again, on the eddying currents of the wind, the bells sang out:

"*Turn–a–gain–Whit–ting–ton!*
Come–back–Dick–Whit–ting–ton!
Lord–Mayor–of–London–town!"

Dick could resist their call no longer. With a sigh that was almost a groan, partly because he did not wish to go back, and partly because he was sorry he had broken his promise and run away, he got up, turned back to the warehouse, and in the early morning crept in through a window, thanking God to find everything safe. And what a scurry and squeaking there was in the back parts of the warehouse when his cat leapt in after him!

So all went well (and better) until the merchant said to Dick one day as he paid him his wages: "Well, Dick, you have been with me for a full year now, and I'm satisfied with you. Now, next week I have a ship sailing for the Indies. Would you like to see the world and go too? The ladies have packed a little chest for you. You shall be cabin boy, and you shall take Puss."

Dick was overjoyed. In a few days the ship put off from the quay and out of the Port of London, gliding over the sparkling Thames (for in those days its waters were clear as crystal and full of fish), and so out to sea. After many weeks of calm and storm, she came in sight at evening of an island ruled by a rich and powerful King named King

Ponmageelza, who had a prodigious store of gold and pearls and precious stones, and huts full of ivory.

Next morning the Captain went ashore to trade with this wealthy potentate. The ship had been sighted by the islanders far out to sea, so the King was ready to receive the Captain, sitting in great splendour under a kind of canopy with his court, while his slaves fanned him with peacocks' plumes. And when the Captain drew near with his sailors he traded with him. He entertained the Captain, too, with good things (though over-rich) to eat and drink.

But while the Captain and Ponmageelza sat there at table, rats were everywhere—long-nosed, ravenous, cunning rascals that gave them not an instant's peace. Such was the impudence of these rats that two of them, even while the Captain's face was turned in talk with the King, scrambled up and nibbled at the yams on his plate. The Captain could scarcely talk or think for the botheration of them, they were so bold and nimble. Indeed, the King had six slaves whose only work it was to keep off the rats.

When the Captain had come back to the ship, Dick heard him talking to the bo'sun and telling him about the rats.

"Such a mort of rats you never set eyes on!" he said. "They'd pick your teeth for you while you eat!" he said. Then Dick made bold to speak up to the Captain:

"If you please, sir, may I go ashore and take my cat with me, and see the King?"

And the Captain said, "Go, my boy; but be back when the gun fires." For Dick had worked hard, and had taken it well when the sailors made sport of him. The Captain liked the lad.

So Dick for safety put his cat into a biscuit bag, after scratching its head and whispering into its ear that all was well, and he was put ashore from the boat, the sea calm and the sands with their tufted palm trees yellow as gold. He came to King Ponmageelza in the heat of the afternoon, and found him lying asleep on a couch, his slaves drowsing on either side of him, and the rats were everywhere. Dick watched them, hardly knowing what to do, standing there, and King Ponmageelza asleep, for he felt Puss scrabbling like half a dozen witches in its bag. But the rats made no more of Dick than a dummy.

Presently, indeed, one of them, even bolder than the rest, having climbed up on to the royal couch, began, as if in sheer bravado, to gnaw at the King's toe, at which the King woke up in a rage and saw Dick standing there. Then Dick ducked his head, and said:

"If you please, your Majesty, I have got something in this bag that will keep down the rats."

But the King merely looked bewildered at this, not understanding a word he said, for Dick spoke English and not in the King's language. So the King sent for an ancient silver-haired man who was a wizard and an interpreter. Dick repeated what he had said about the rats, and the wizard told and interpreted to the King what Dick had said. And the King said, "Oh!"

Then Dick showed the King what he had in his biscuit bag. Indeed, the very instant he loosened the string of the bag Puss sprang out with a growl like a ghollie-grampus, the first growl Dick had ever heard it utter, and before you could say Jack Robinson seventeen rats lay stricken on the floor, and the rest had scuttled back into their runs. If this was mere day-work, what of the night?

The King was pleased beyond measure. His black face shone with joy, and he said he would buy the cat. But Dick shook his head. He would lend his cat, but not sell. The King still wished, but Dick kept on and wouldn't, and said, "No." At length it was agreed between them that King Ponmageelza should borrow and keep the cat for one whole year, and for this the King promised to give Dick twelve casks of gold and silver and precious stones, and a good bundle of tusks of ivory. It seemed to Dick he was getting a marvellous good price for the loan of his cat, but the King, having more of these things than was any good to him, thought it a bargain.

At that moment the gun sounded from the ship, and Dick, having bidden Puss goodbye, went down to the beach where there was a boat waiting for him. It was getting to evening now, but not yet dark. He told the sailors to fetch twelve empty casks; so the sailors rowed back to the ship and brought back the empty casks, and the King's slaves filled them with gold and silver and precious stones, and then carried down the bundles of ivory. Three times the sailors rowed back and forth (from the ship), and the last time in the pitch-dark, though the sea was milky-green with a light like phosphorus in the water and the tropic stars were blazing.

When Dick reached England again, and the ship had sailed up the Thames to the wharf he knew so well, the merchant heard his tale to the end, and was delighted with his good fortune.

"See here, Master Whittington," he said clapping him friendly on the shoulder, "You and I will trade together, and if you do well you shall marry my daughter, and when I die you shall be my heir."

And Dick, who owed all his good fortune to his master, blushed and said, "Yes." Of his own free will— and glad he was to do it—he gave the merchant two of the casks cramful of the mixture of what he had had from Ponmageelza, and seven tusks of the best of his ivory. This was a present. After that he picked out from what was left enough great pearls for a necklace that would go round a slender neck, and he gave this to his master's daughter. At which she blushed more even than Dick had. After that he worked harder than ever.

At the end of the year, when the ship came back again from her voyage to the Indies, the Captain brought with him Dick's cat, more sleek and shapely than ever, and wearing a collar of sharkskin studded with emeralds round its neck, and these sewed in with elephant's hair. When Dick took Puss into his arms again he couldn't keep the tears out of his eyes; and Puss nuzzled his face and purred.

For a present, and simply in gratitude for the cat, the black King had sent Dick twelve more casks of precious stones, and another great clump of elephants' tusks, some of them carved with animals and palms. So Dick and his master prospered more and more, until in due time Dick married his master's daughter, whose name was Alice, became himself London's greatest of merchants, and at last Lord Mayor.

On the very day he became Lord Mayor, as he sat in his coach, rolling over the cobbles, with the great gold mace at the window, the bells clanging in the steeples, and the people huzzaing from the streets, windows and housetops, he went back in thought to the ragged boy called Dick who had come with only his cat out of the country to the great city and was now Sir Richard Whittington, the most beloved of her freemen, and a friend of the King himself. I say, as he sat in his coach listening to the bells, he heard no more the shouting and huzzaing of the people, but only what the bells in their distant chimes had said to him years and years ago, that spring daybreak on the hill of Highgate, when by night he had run away out of the warehouse:

"Turn–a–gain–Whit–ting–ton!
Come–back–Dick–Whit–ting–ton!
Lord–Mayor–of–London–town!"

He rejoiced at thought of it, yet at the same moment felt quiet and humble.

When he got back to his mansion in the city, and before he made himself ready for the great banquet that evening, he gave his cat, who was now, alas! long past mousing, a tender young roast pigeon for its supper—a pigeon specially stuffed and garnished with rats'-tails. He had the bird served, too, on a silver platter—though Puss as soon as he set teeth into it pulled it off on to the floor. At sight of this, Lady Whittington, who stood beside him, kissed Dick on both cheeks and laughed out loud. Nor was Dick chosen Mayor of London but once. He was Mayor four times, was loved and revered by all men in the city, and famous not only in England but far and wide.

Cinderella and the Glass Slipper

───────◦❉◦───────

There were once upon a time three sisters who lived in an old, high, stone house in a street not very far from the great square of the city where was the palace of the King. The two eldest of these sisters were old and ugly, which is bad enough. They were also sour and jealous, which is worse. And simply because the youngest (who was only their half-sister) was gentle and lovely, they hated her.

While they themselves sat in comfort in their fine rooms upstairs, she was made to live in a dark, stone-flagged kitchen with nothing but rats, mice, and cockroaches for company. There, in a kind of cupboard, she slept. By day she did the housework—cooking and scrubbing and sweeping and scouring. She made the beds, she washed their linen, she darned their stockings, she mended their clothes. She was never in bed till midnight; and, summer or winter, she had to be up every morning at five, to fetch water, to chop up the firewood and light the fires. In the blind, frozen mornings of winter she could scarcely creep about for the cold.

Yet, in spite of all this, though she hadn't enough to eat, though her sisters never wearied of nagging and scolding at her, or of beating her, either, when they felt in the humour, she soon forgot their tongues and bruises.

She must have been happy by nature, just as by nature a may-tree is covered with leaves and blossom, or water jets out of a well-spring. To catch sight of a sunbeam lighting up the kitchen wall now and then, or the moon-light stealing across the floor, or merely to wake and hear the birds shrilling at daybreak, was enough to set her heart on fire.

She would jump out of bed, say her prayers, slip into her rags, wash her bright face under the pump, comb her dark hair; then, singing too, not like the birds, but softly under her breath, would begin her work. Sometimes she would set herself races against the old kitchen clock; or say to herself, "When I've done this and this and this and *this*, I'll look out of the window." However late it was before the day was finished, she made it a rule always to sit for a little while in front of the great kitchen fire, her stool drawn close up to the hearth among the cinders. There she would begin to dream even before she fell alseep; and in mockery her sisters called her Cinderella.

They never left her at peace. If they could not find work for her to do, they made it; and for food gave her their crusts and bits left over. They hated her, and hated her all the more because, in spite of their scowls and grumblings, she never stayed mumpish or sulky, while her cheeks ever grew fairer and her eyes brighter. She couldn't help it. Since she felt young and happy, she couldn't but seem so.

Now all this may have been in part because Cinderella had a fairy godmother. This fairy godmother had come to her christening, and well the sisters remembered it. This little bunched-up old woman had a hump on her back, was dressed in outlandish clothes and a high steeple hat, and the two impudent trollops (who even then tried to make themselves look younger than they were) had called her "Old Stump-Stump", had put out their tongues at her, and laughed at every word she said.

But, except for one slow piercing look at them out of her green eyes (after which they laughed no more), the old woman had paid them no heed. She had stooped over Cinderella's wooden cradle and gazed a long time at her sleeping face, then, laying her skinny fore-finger on the mite's chin, she had slowly nodded—once, twice, thrice. If every nod meant a fairy gift, then what wonder Cinderella had cheeks like a wild rose, eyes clear as dewdrops, and a tongue like a blackbird's?

Now Cinderella, of course, could not remember her christening; and her godmother had never been seen or heard of since. She seemed to have quite forgotten her godchild; and when one day Cinderella spoke of her to her sisters, they were beside themselves with rage.

"Godmother, forsooth!" they cackled. "Crazy old humpback! Much she cares for you, Miss Slut! Keep to your cinders; and no more drowsing and dreaming by the fire!"

So time went on, until at last Cinderella was so used to their pinchings and beatings and scoldings that she hardly noticed them. She kept out of their company as much as she could, almost forgot how to cry, was happy when she was alone, and was never idle.

Now a little before Christmas in the year when Cinderella was eighteen, the King sent out his trumpeters to proclaim that on Twelfth Night there was to be a great Ball at the Palace, with such dancing and feasting and revelry as had never been known in that country before. Bonfires were to be lit on the hills, torches in the streets. There were to be stalls of hot pies, eels, sweetmeats, cakes and comfits in the market-place. There were to be booths showing strange animals and birds and suchlike; and the fountains in the city were to run that night with wine. For the next day after it would be the twenty-first birthday of the King's only son. When the people heard the proclamation of the King's trumpeters, there were wild rejoicings, and they at once began to make ready for the feast.

In due time there came to the old stone house where the three sisters lived the King's Lord Chamberlain. At sound of the wheels of his coach the two elder sisters squinnied down out of their window and then at once scuttled downstairs to lock Cinderella up in the kitchen, in case he should see not only her rags, but her lovely young face. He had come, as they guessed, to bring them the King's command that they should attend the great Ball. "I see, madam, three are invited," he said, looking at his scroll.

"Ay," said they, as if in grief, "but only two of us are left." So he bowed and withdrew.

After that the two old sisters scarcely stopped talking about the Ball. They could think of nothing else. They spent the whole day and every day in turning out their chests and wardrobes in search of whatever bit of old finery they could lay hands on. For hours together they sat in front of their great looking-glass, smirking this way and languishing that, trying on any old gown or cloak they could find—slippers and sashes, wigs and laces and buckles and necklaces, and never of the same mind for two minutes together. And when they weren't storming at Cinderella, they were quarrelling and wrangling between themselves.

As for Cinderella, from morning to night she sat stitching and stitching till she could scarcely see out of her young eyes or hold her needle. The harder she worked and the more she tried to please them, the worse they fumed and flustered. They were like wasps in a trap.

At last came the night of the Ball. The streets were ablaze with torches and bonfires. In every window burned wax tapers. Shawls and silks of all the colours of the rainbow dangled from sill and balcony. Wine red and golden gushed from the fountains. Everywhere there was feasting and merriment, laughter and music. At one end of the city was a booth of travelling bears, which were soon so crammed with buns and honeycomb that they could only sit and pant; and at the other was a troupe of Barbary apes that played on every kind of instrument of music. Besides which, there was a singing Mermaid; a Giant, with a dwarf on his hat-brim; and a wild man from the Indies that gulped down flaming pitch as if it were milk and water.

The country people, all in their best and gayest clothes (and they came from far and near as if to a Fair), had brought their children even to the youngest, and stood gazing and gaping at the dressed-up lords and ladies in their coaches and carriages on their way to the Palace. There were coaches with six horses, and coaches with four; and a fat, furred, scarlet-silked postillion to each pair. The whole city under the tent of the starry night flared bright as a peepshow.

But Cinderella hadn't a moment even to peer down from an upper window at these wonders. She hardly knew whether she was on her head or her heels. And when her two old sisters—looking in their wigs and powder more like bunched-up fantastic monkeys than human beings—had at last rolled off in their hired carriage to the Palace, she was so tired she could scarcely creep upstairs.

After tidying up the litter in their bedrooms, and making a pot of soup to be kept simmering for them till they came home, she drew her stool up to the kitchen fire, with not even the heart to look out of the window. She had never before felt so lonely or wretched, and as she sat there in the red glow of the smouldering coals, before even she knew it was there, a tear rolled down her cheek and splashed with a sizzle into the hot ashes. She ached all over. Nevertheless she poked up the fire again, swept up the ashes, began to sing a little to herself, forgot to go on, and as she did so set to wondering what *she* would be doing now if she herself had gone to the Palace. "But since you can't be in two places at once, my dear," she suddenly laughed out loud, "why here you must stay."

By now it had grown quieter in the streets, and against the black of the window in the wintry night snow was falling. Sitting on her stool among the cinders, Cinderella listened to the far-away strains of music. But these too died away as she listened; utter silence came with the snow; and in a minute or two she would have fallen fast asleep.

Indeed, all was so hushed at last in the vacant kitchen that the ashes, like pygmy bells in a belfry, tinkled as they fell; a cricket began shrilly churring from a crevice in the hob, and she could hear the tiny *tic-a-tac-tac* of the mice as they came tippeting and frisking round her stool. Then, suddenly, softly, and without warning, there sounded out of the deep hush a gentle knock-knocking at the door.

Cinderella's drowsy eyes opened wide. The mice scuttled to their wainscot. Then all was still again. What stranger was this, come in the dark and the snow? Maybe, thought Cinderella, it was only the wind in the ivy. But no, yet again there sounded that gentle knocking—there could be no mistake of that. So Cinderella rose from her stool, lit the tallow candle in an old copper candlestick, and, lifting the latch, peered out into the night.

The stars of huge Orion were wildly shaking in the dark hollow of the sky; the cold air lapped her cheek; and the garden was mantled deep and white as wool with snow. And behold on the doorstep stood a little old humpbacked woman, with a steeple hat on her head, and over her round shoulders a buckled green cloak that came down to her very heels.

"Good evening, my dear," said the old woman. "I see you don't know who *I* am?" Her green eyes gleamed in the candlelight as she peered into the gloom of the kitchen. "And why, pray, are you sitting here alone, when all the world is gone to the Ball?"

Cinderella looked at her—at her green far-set eyes and long hooked nose, and she smiled back at the old woman and begged her to come in. Then she told her about the Ball.

"Ahai!" said the old woman, "and I'll be bound to say, my dear, you'd like to go too. Ay, so I thought. Come, then, there's no time to waste. Night's speeding on. Put on your gown and we'll be off to the Palace at once."

Now her sisters had strictly forbidden Cinderella to stir from the house in their absence. Bread and water for three days they had threatened her with if she so much as opened the door. But she knew in her heart they had not told her the truth about the Ball. She knew she had been invited to go too; and now she was not so frightened of them as she used to be. None the less, she could only smile in reply to the old woman, and all she could say was: "It's very very kind of you, ma'am. I should dearly like to go to the Ball, and I'm sorry; but I've nothing to go in."

Now the old woman was carrying in her hand (for she stooped nearly double) a crutch or staff, and she said,

"Ahai! my dear! Rags and skin, eh? So it's nothing but a gown you need. *That's* soon mended."

With that, she lifted a little her crutch into the air, and as if at a sign and as if an owl had swooped in out of the night, there floated in through the open door out of the darkness and snow a small square Arabian leather trunk, red and gold, with silver hinges and a silver lock.

The old woman touched the lock with her crutch and the lid flew open. And beneath the lid there lay a gown of spangled orient muslin edged with swansdown and seed pearls and white as hoar-frost. There was a fan of strange white feathers, too, and a wreath of green leaves and snow-flowers, such flowers as bloom only on the tops of mountains under the stars.

"So there's the gown!" said the old woman with a cackle. "Now hasten, my dear. Polish up those bright young cheeks of yours, and we'll soon get a-going."

Cinderella ran off at once into the scullery, put her face under the pump, and scrubbed away until her cheeks were like wild roses, and her hands like cuckoo-flowers. She came back combing her hair with all that was left of her old comb, and then and there, in front of the kitchen fire, shook herself free of her rags and slipped into the muslin gown. Whereupon she looked exactly like a rose-bush dazzling with hoar-frost under the moon.

The old woman herself laced up the silver laces, and herself with a silver pin pinned the wreath of green leaves and snow-flowers in Cinderella's dark hair, then kissed her on both cheeks. As they stood there together, yet again the far-away music of fiddle and trumpet came stealing in through the night air from the Palace. And suddenly Cinderella frowned, and a shadow stole over her face.

"But look, ma'am," said she, "just look at my old

shoes!" For there they stood, both of them together by the hearth, two old battered clouts that had long been friends in need and in deed, but had by now seen far too much of the world. The old woman laughed and stooped over them.

"Why," she said, "what's being old, my dear? Merely little by little, and less by less." As she said these words, she jerked up the tip of her crutch again, and, behold, the two old patched-up shoes seemed to have floated off into another world and come back again. For in their stead was a pair of slippers the like of which Cinderella had never seen or even dreamed of. They were of spun glass and lined with swansdown, and Cinderella slipped her ten toes into them as easily as a minnow slips under a stone.

"Oh, Godmother! Look!" she cried. "And now I am ready!"

"Ahai!" said the old woman, pleased to her very heart-strings with her happy young god-daughter. "And how, pray, are we going to get through the snow?"

"I think, do you know, dear Godmother," said Cinderella, frowning a little, "I should love to *walk*." Her Godmother pointed with her crutch, and, looking at Cinderella with her sharp green eyes, said:

> "*Never grumbling, nought awry;*
> Always willing *asks no why;*
> *Patient waiting, free as air—*
> *What's that pumpkin over there?*"

Then Cinderella looked at the old summer pumpkin in the corner by the dresser that had been put by for pie in the winter, and didn't know what to say.

"Bring it a little closer, my dear," said her Godmother. So Cinderella lifted the great pumpkin in her bare arms and laid it down by the hearth. Once more the old woman waved her crutch, and, behold, the pumpkin swelled and swelled before Cinderella's very eyes; it swelled in its faded mottled green till it was as huge as a puncheon of wine, and then split softly open. And before Cinderella could so much as sigh with surprise and delight, there, on its snow-slides, stood a small, round-topped, green and white coach.

"Ahai!" breathed the old woman again, and out of their holes came scampering a round dozen of house mice, which, with yet another wave of her crutch, were at once transformed into twelve small deer, like gazelles, with silver antlers, and harness of silver, bridles and reins. Six of them stood out in the snow under the stars, four of them in the kitchen, and two in the entry. Then out from a larger hole under the shelf where the pots and pans were kept, and behind which was the stone larder with its bacon and cheeses, brisked four smart black rats; and these also were changed and transmogrified as if at a whisper, and now sat up on the coach, two in front and two behind—a sharp-nosed coachman and three dapper footmen. And the coachman sat with the long reins in his hand, waiting for Cinderella to get in.

Then the old woman said:

"And now, my dear, I must leave you. There's but one thing you must remember. Be sure to hasten away from the Palace before the clock has finished tolling twelve. Midnight, my dear. The coach will be waiting, and you must haste away home."

Cinderella looked at her Godmother, and for the second time that evening a tear rolled glittering down her cheek. Oddly enough, though this was a tear of happiness, it was *exactly* like the tear that had rolled down her cheek in her wretchedness as she sat alone.

"Oh, dear, dear Godmother, how can I thank you?" she said.

"Well, my dear," said the old woman, "if you don't know how, why, you can't. And if you can't, why, you needn't." And she kissed her once more.

Then Cinderella stepped into the coach. The old woman lifted her crutch. The coachman cracked his whip. The deer, with their silver clashing antlers and silver harness, scooped in the snow their slender hoofs, and out of the kitchen off slid the coach into a silence soft as wool. On, on, under the dark starry sky into streets still flaming and blazing with torches and bonfires, it swept, bearing inside of it not only the last of the King's guests, but by far the loveliest. As for the people still abroad, at sight of it and of Cinderella they opened their mouths in the utmost astonishment, then broke into a loud huzza. But Cinderella heard not a whisper—she was gone in a flash.

When she appeared in the great ball-room, thronged with splendour, its flowers vying in light with its thousands of wax candles in sconce and chandelier, even the fiddlers stopped bowing an instant to gaze at such a wonder. Even so much as one peep at Cinderella was a joy and marvel.

The Prince himself came down from the dais where sat his father and mother, and himself led Cinderella to the throne. They danced together once, they danced together twice, and yet again. And Cinderella, being so happy and lovely, and without scorn, pride or vanity in her face, everyone there delighted to watch her, except only her two miserable half-sisters, who sat in a corner under a bunch of mistletoe and glared at her in envy and rage.

Not that they even dreamed who she was. No, even though they were her half-sisters, and had lived in the

same house with her since she was a child. But then, who could have supposed this was the slattern and drudge they had left at home among her cinders?

But how swiftly slips time away when the heart is happy! The music, the radiant tapers, the talking and feasting—the hours melted like hoar-frost in the sun. And even while Cinderella was once more dancing with the Prince, his dark eyes looking as if he himself were half a-dream, Cinderella heard again the great bell of the Palace clock begin to toll: *One—two—three* . . .

"Oh!" she sighed, and her heart seemed to stand still, "I hear a clock!"

And the Prince said: "Never heed the clock. It is telling us only how little time we have, and how well we should use it." *Five—six—seven* . . .

But "Oh!" Cinderella said, "what time is it telling?"

And the Prince said, "Midnight."

With that, all the colour ebbed out of her young cheeks. She drew herself away from the Prince, and ran off as fast as her feet could carry her. Straight out of the ball-room she scampered, down the long corridor, down yet another, and down the marble staircase. But as she turned at the foot of the staircase, she stumbled a little, and her left slipper slipped off. Cinderella could not wait. Eleven strokes had sounded, and as she leapt breathlessly into the coach there boomed out the twelfth. She was not a moment too soon.

Presently after, yet as if in no time, she found herself at home again in the cold black kitchen. Nothing was changed, though the fire was out, the candle but a stub. There in its corner by the potboard lay the pumpkin. And here as of old sat she herself, shivering a little in her rags on her three-legged stool among the cinders, and only the draughty door ajar and a few tiny plumes of swansdown on the flagstones for proof that she had ever stirred from the house.

But for these, all that had passed might have been a dream. But Cinderella was far too happy for that to be true, and her face was smiling as she looked into the cold ashes of the fire. She looked and she pondered; and while she was pondering, it was as if a voice had asked her a question, "Why is your foot so cold?"

She looked down, and to her dismay saw on one foot a glass slipper, and on the other nothing but an old black stocking. The old woman's magic had come and gone, but it had forgotten a slipper. And even while Cinderella was thinking what she should do, there came a loud pealing of the bell above her head, and she knew that her sisters had come back from the Ball.

So, one foot shod and one foot stockinged, she hastened upstairs with the soup, and helped her sisters to get to bed. Never before had they been in such a rage. Nothing she could do was right. They pinched her when she came near, and flung their slippers at her when she went away; and she soon knew what was amiss. They could talk of nothing else but the strange princess (as they thought her) who had come late to the Ball and with her witcheries had enchanted not only the young Prince but even the King and Queen and the whole Court, down to the very dwarfs, imps, and pages. Their tired old eyes squinted with envy, and they seemed so worn-out and wretched that Cinderella longed to comfort them if only but just to say: "But why trouble about her? *She* will never come back again."

She was thankful at any rate they were too busy with their tongues to notice her feet; and at last she slipped downstairs, *clip-clop, clip-clop,* and was soon safe in bed and asleep.

The very next day the royal trumpeters were trumpeting in the streets once more. Even the Prince had not been able to run as fast as Cinderella, and had come out into the snowy night only just in time to see her coach of magic vanish into the dark. But he had picked up her slipper as he came back.

Proclamation was sounded that anyone who should bring tidings of this lovely young stranger or of her slipper, should be richly rewarded. But Cinderella in her kitchen heard not even an echo of the trumpeters. So they trumpeted in vain.

Then the King sent out his Lord Chamberlain with six pages to attend him. They were bidden search through the city, house by house. And one of the pages carried before the Lord Chamberlain the glass slipper on a crimson cushion with tassels of pearls. At each house in turn, every lady in it was bidden try on the slipper, for the King was determined to find its owner, unless indeed she was of the undiscoverable Courts of Faërie. For most of the ladies the slipper was too high in the instep; for many it was too narrow in the tread; and for all it was far too short.

At last, the Lord Chamberlain came to the house of the three sisters. The two old sisters had already heard what passed when the page brought in the slipper. So the elder of them with a pair of tailor's shears had snipped off a big toe, and bound up her foot with a bandage. But even this was of no avail. For when she tried, in spite of the pain, to push her foot into it, the slipper was far too narrow. The second sister also, with a great cook's knife, had secretly carved off a piece of her heel, and had bound that foot up with a bandage. But even this was of no avail. For push and pull as she might, the shoe was at least an inch too short.

The Lord Chamberlain looked angrily at the sisters.

"Is there any other lady dwelling in this house?" he said.

The two sisters narrowed their eyes one at the other, and lied and said, "No." Yet even at that very moment there welled in a faint singing as if out of the very bowels of the earth.

The Lord Chamberlain said, "What voice is that I hear?"

The two sisters almost squinted as they glanced again each at the other, and the one said it was a tame popinjay and the other that it was the creaking of the pump.

"Then," said the Lord Chamberlain, "the pump has learned English!" He at once sent two of his pages to seek out the singer whose voice he had heard, and to bring her into his presence. So Cinderella had to appear before him in her rags, just as she was. But when she saw the glass slipper on the crimson cushion, she almost laughed out loud.

The Lord Chamberlain, marvelling at her beauty, said: "Why do you smile, my child?"

She said, "Because, my lord, I have a slipper exactly like that one myself. It's in a drawer in the kitchen dresser." And when one of the pages had brought the other slipper, behold, Cinderella's two feet with both their heels and all their ten toes slipped into them as easily as a titmouse into its nest.

When Cinderella was brought to the King and the Queen, they received her as if she were a long-lost daughter. Far and near, once more, at her wedding, the bonfires blazed all night among the hills, the fountains in the market-place ran with wine: there were stalls of venison pies, black puddings and eels, sweetmeats, cakes and comfits, and such a concourse of strangers and noblemen in the city as it had never contained before.

Of Cinderella's guests of honour the first was a hum-pity-backed old woman muffled up in a green mantle, who ate nothing, and drank nothing, and said nothing; but smiled and smiled and smiled.

As for the elder sisters, they sat at home listening to the wedding bells clashing their changes in the steeples. The one being without a heel to her left foot, and the other without a big toe, they walked lame ever afterwards. And their neighbours, laughing at their folly, called them the Two Old Stump-stumps.

The Dancing Princesses

There was a King of old who had twelve daughters. Some of them were fair as swans in spring, some dark as trees on a mountain-side, and all were beautiful. And because the King wished to keep their beauty to himself only, they slept at night in twelve beds in one long, stone chamber, whose doors were closely barred and bolted.

Yet, in spite of this, as soon as the year came round to May again, and the stars and cold of winter were gone and the world was merry, at morning and every morning the soles of the twelve Princesses' slippers were found to be worn through to the very welts. It was as if they must have been dancing in them all the night long.

News of this being brought to the King, he marvelled. Unless they had wings, how could they have flown out of the Palace? There was neither crevice nor cranny in the heavy doors. He spied. He set watch. It made no difference. Brand-new though the Princesses' gold and silver slippers were overnight, they were worn-out at morning. He was in rage and despair.

At last this King made a decree. He decreed that anyone who, by waking and watching, by wisdom or magic, should reveal this strange secret, and where and how and when the twelve Princesses' slippers went of nights to get so worn, he should have the hand in marriage of whichever one of the Princesses he chose, and should be made the heir to the throne. As for anyone foolish enough to be so bold as to attempt such a task and fail in it, he should be whipped out of the kingdom, and maybe lose his ears into the bargain. But, such was the beauty of these Princesses, many a high-born stranger lost, not only his heart, but his ears also; and the King grew ever more moody and morose.

Now beyond the walls of the royal house where lived the twelve Princesses was a forest; and one summer's evening an old soldier who was travelling home from the wars met there, on his way, a beldame with a pig. This old beldame had brought her pig to the forest to feed on the beech-mast and truffles, but now, try as she might, she could not prevail upon it to be caught and to return home with her to its sty. She would steal up behind it with its cord in her hand, but as soon as she drew near and all but in touch of it, the pig, that meanwhile had been busily rooting in the cool loose loam, with a flick of its ears and a twinkle of its tail, would scamper off out of her reach. It was almost as if its little sharp glass-green eyes could see through the pink shutters of its ears.

The old soldier watched the pig (and the red sunlight was glinting in the young green leaves of the beeches), and at last he said: "If I may make so bold, Grannie, I know a little secret about pigs. And if, as I take it, you want to catch *that* particular pig, it's yours and welcome."

The beldame, who had fingers like birds' claws and eyes black as sloes, thanked the old soldier. Fetching out a scrap of some secret root from the bottom of his knapsack, he first slowly turned his back on the pig, then stooped down and, with the bit of root between his teeth, stared earnestly at the pig from between his legs.

Presently, either by reason of the savour of the root or drawn by curiosity, the pig edged closer and closer to the old soldier, until at last it actually came nosing and sidling in underneath him, as if under a bridge. Then in a trice the old soldier snatched him up by ear and tail, and slipped the noose of the cord fast. The pig squealed like forty demons, but more as if in fun than in real rage.

"There we are, Grannie," said the old soldier, giving the old beldame her pig, "and here's a scrap of the root, too. There's no pig all the world over, white, black, or piebald, but after he gets one sniff of it comes for more. *That* I'll warrant you, and I'm sure you're very welcome."

The beldame, with her pig now safely at the rope's end and the scrap of root between her fingers, thanked the old soldier and asked him of his journey and whither he was going; and it was just as if, with its snout uplifted, its ears drawn forward, the nimble young pig was also listening for his answer.

The old soldier told her he was returning from the wars. "But as for where *to*, Grannie, or what for, I hardly know. For wife or children have I none, and most of my old friends must have long ago forgotten me. Not that I'm meaning to say, Grannie," says the soldier, "that *that* much matters, me being come so far, and no turning back. Still, there's just *one* thing I'd like to find out before I go, and that is where the twelve young daughters of the mad old King yonder dance of nights. If I knew that, Grannie, they say I might some day sit on a throne." With that he burst out laughing, at which the pig, with a twist of its jaws (as though recalling the sweet savour of the root), flung up its three-cornered head and laughed too.

The beldame, eyeing the old soldier closely, said that

what he had asked was not a hard or dangerous matter, if only he would promise to do exactly what she told him. The old soldier found *that* easy enough.

"Well," said the beldame, "when you come to the Palace, you'll be set to watch, and you'll be tempted to sleep. Vow a vow, then, to taste not even a crumb of the sweet cake or sip so much as a sip of the wine the Princesses will bring to you before they go to bed. Wake and watch; then follow where they lead; and here is a cloak which, come fair or foul, will make you invisible." At this the beldame took a cloak finer than spider silk from out of a small bag or pouch she wore, and gave it him.

"That hide me!" said the soldier. "Old coat, brass buttons, and all?"

"Ay," said the beldame, and thanked him again for his help; and the pig coughed, and so they parted.

When she was out of sight the old soldier had another look at the magic cloak, and thought over what the beldame had told him. Being by nature bold and brave, and having nothing better to do, he went off at once to the King.

The King looked at the old soldier, listened to what he said, and then with a grim smile half-hidden under his beard, bade him follow him to a little stone closet hard by the long chamber where the Princesses slept. "Watch here," he said, "and if you can discover this secret, then the reward I have decreed shall be yours. If not——" He glanced up under his brows at the brave old soldier (who had no more fear in his heart than he had money in his pocket), but did not finish his sentence.

A little before nightfall, the old soldier sat himself down on a bench in the stone closet, and by the light of a stub of candle began to mend his shoe.

By-and-by the eldest of the Princesses knocked softly

on his door, smiled on him and brought him a cup of wine and a dish of sweet cakes. He thanked her. But as soon as she was gone he dribbled out the wine drip by drip into a hole between the flagstones, and made crumbs of the cakes for the mice. Then he lay down and pretended to be asleep. He snored and snored, but even while he snored he was busy with his cobbler's awl boring a little hole for a peephole between the stone of the wall where he lay and the Princesses' room. At midnight all was still.

But hardly had the little owl of midnight called, *Ahoo! ahoo! ahoo!* when the old soldier, hearing a gentle stirring in the next room, peeped through the tiny hole he had bored in the wall. His eyes dazzled; a wondrous sight was to be seen. For the Princesses in the filmy silver of the moon were now dressing and attiring themselves in clothes that seemed not of this world, but from some strange otherwhere, which they none the less took out of their own coffers and wardrobes. They seemed to be as happy as larks in the morning, or like swallows chittering before they fly, laughing and whispering together while they put on these bright garments and made ready. Only one of them, the youngest, had withdrawn herself a little apart and delayed to join them, and now kept silent. Seeing this, her sisters made merry at her, and asked her what ailed her.

"The others," she said, "whom our father set to watch us were young and foolish. But that old soldier has wandered all over the world and has seen many things, and it seems to me he is crafty and wise. That, sisters, is why I say, Beware!"

Still they only laughed at her. "Crafty and wise, forsooth!" said they. "Listen to his snoring! He has eaten of our sweet cakes and drunken the spiced wine, and now he will sleep sound till morning." At this the old soldier,

peeping through his little bore-hole in the stones, smiled to himself, and went on snoring.

When they were all ready to be gone, the eldest of the Princesses clapped her hands. At this signal, and as if by magic, in the middle of the floor one wide flagstone wheeled softly upon its neighbour, disclosing an opening there, and beneath it a narrow winding flight of steps. One by one, according to age, the Princesses followed the eldest down this secret staircase, and the old soldier knew there was no time to be lost.

He flung the old beldame's cloak over his shoulders, and (as she had foretold) instantly of himself there showed not even so much as a shadow. Then, having noiselessly unbarred the door into the Princesses' bedroom, he followed the youngest of them down the stone steps.

It was dark beneath the flagstones, and the old soldier trod clumsily in his heavy shoes. And as he groped down he stumbled, and trod on the hem of the youngest Princess's dress.

"Alas, sisters, a hand is clutching at me!" she called out to her sisters.

"A hand!" mocked the eldest. "You must have caught your sleeve on a nail!"

On and down they went, and out of a narrow corridor at last emerged and came full into the open air, and following a faint track in the green turf, reached at last a wood where the trees (their bark, branches, twigs and leaves) were all of silver and softly shimmering in a gentle light that seemed to be neither of sun nor moon nor stars. Anon they came to a second wood, and here the trees shone softly too, but these were of gold. Anon they came to a third wood, and here the trees were in fruit, and the fruits upon them were precious stones—green, blue, and amber, and burning orange.

When the Princesses had all passed through this third wood, they broke out upon a hillside, and, looking down from out the leaf-fringed trees, the old soldier saw the calm waters of a lake beyond yellow sands, and drawn up on its strand twelve swan-shaped boats. And there, standing as if in wait beside them, were twelve young men that looked to be Princes. Noble and handsome young men they were.

The Princesses, having hastened down to the strand, greeted these young men one and all, and at once embarked into the twelve swan-shaped boats, the old soldier smuggling himself as gingerly as he could into the boat of the youngest. Then the Princes rowed away softly across the water towards an island that was in the midst of the lake, where was a Palace, its windows shining like crystal in the wan light that bathed sky and water.

Only the last of the boats lagged far behind the others, for the old soldier sitting there invisible on the thwart, though little else but bones and sinews, weighed as heavy as a sack of stones in the boat. At last the youngest of the Princes leaned on his oars to recover his breath. "What," he sighed, "can be amiss with this boat to-night? It never rowed so heavily."

The youngest of the Princesses looked askance at him with fear in her eyes, for the boat was atilt with the weight of the old soldier and not trimmed true. Whereupon she turned her small head and looked towards that part of the boat where sat the old soldier, for there it dipped deepest in the water. In so doing, she gazed straight into his eyes, yet perceived nothing but the green water beyond. He smiled at her, and—though she knew not why—she was comforted. "Maybe," she said, turning to the Prince again and answering what he had said— "maybe you are wearied because of the heat of the evening." And he rowed on.

When they were come to the island and into the Palace there, the old soldier could hardly believe his eyes, it was a scene so fair and strange and unearthly. All the long night through, to music of harp and tambour and pipe, the Princesses danced with the Princes. Danced, too, the fountains at play, with an endless singing of birds, trees with flowers blossoming, and no-one seemed to weary. But as soon as the scarlet shafts of morning showed beyond these skies, they returned at once to the boats, and the Princesses were soon back safely under the King's roof again, and so fast asleep in their beds that they looked as if they had never stirred or even sighed in them the whole night long. They might be lovely images of stone.

But the old soldier slept like a hare—with one eye open.

When he awoke, which was soon, he began to think over all that he had seen and heard. The longer he pondered on it, the more he was filled with astonishment. Every now and then, as if to make sure of the land of the living, he peeped with his eye through the hole in the wall, for he was almost of a mind to believe that his journey of the night before—the enchanted woods, the lake, the Palace and the music—was nothing more than the make-believe of a dream.

So, being a man of caution, he determined to say nothing at all of what had passed this first night, but to watch again a second night. When dark drew on, he once more dribbled out the spiced wine into the crannies of the stones and crumbled the sweet cakes into morsels for the mice, himself eating nothing but a crust or two of rye-bread and a rind of cheese that he had in his haversack.

All happened as before. Midnight came. The Princesses rose up out of their beds, gay and brisk as fish leaping at evening out of their haunts, and soon had made ready and were gone to their trysting-place at the lake-side. All was as before.

The old soldier—to make sure even surer—watched for the third night. But this night, as he followed the Princesses, first through the wood where the leaves were of silver, and next where they resembled fine gold, and last where the fruits on the boughs were all of precious stones, he broke off in each a twig. As he did so, the third time, the tree faintly sighed, and the youngest Princess heard the tree sigh. Her fears of the first night, far from being lulled and at rest, had only grown sharper. She stayed a moment in the wood, looking back, and cried, "Sisters! Sisters! We are being watched. We are being followed. I heard this tree sigh, and it was in warning." But they only laughed at her.

"Sigh, forsooth!" they said. "So, too, would you, sister, if you were clad in leaves as trees are, and a little wind went through your branches."

Hearing this, in hope to reassure her, the old soldier softly wafted the three twigs he carried in the air at a little distance from the youngest's face. Sweet was the scent of them, and she smiled. That night, too, for further proof, the old soldier stole one of the gold drinking-cups in the Princes' Palace and hid it away with the twigs in his haversack. Then for the last time he watched the dancing, and listened to the night birds' music and the noise of the fountains. But being tired, he sat down and yawned, for he had no great wish to be young again, and was happy in being himself.

Indeed, as he looked in at the Princesses, fast, fast asleep that third early morning, their dreamless faces lying waxen and placid amid the braids of their long hair upon their pillows, he even pitied them.

That very day he asked to be taken before the King, and when he was come into his presence entreated of him a favour.

"Say on!" said the King. The old soldier then besought the King to promise that if he told the secret thing he had discovered, he would forgive the Princesses all that had gone before.

"I'd rather," he said, "be whipped three times round your Majesty's kingdom than open my mouth else."

The King promised. Then the old soldier brought out from his haversack the three twigs of the trees—the silver and the gold and the begemmed—and the gold cup from the banqueting hall; and he told the King all that had befallen him.

On first hearing of this, the King fell into a rage at the thought of how his daughters had deceived him. But he remembered his promise and was pacified. He remembered, too, the decree he had made, and sent word that his daughters should be bidden into his presence. When they were come, the dark and the fair together, he frowned on them, then turned to the old soldier: "Now choose which of these deceivers you will have for wife, for such was my decree."

The old soldier, looking at them each in turn, and smiling at the youngest, waved his great hand and said: "My liege, there is this to be said: Never lived any man high or low that *deserved* a wife as gentle and fair as one of these. But in the place of enchantment I have told of, there were twelve young Princes. Well-spoken and soldierly young men they were; and if it was choosing sons I was, such are the sons I would choose. As for myself, now—if I may be so bold, and if it would be any ease to your Majesty's mind—it being a promise, in a manner of speaking—there's one thing, me having roved the world over all my life, I'm mortal anxious to *know*——" and here he paused.

"Say on," said the King.

"Why," replied the old soldier, "what sort of thing it feels like to sit, even though but for the mite of a moment, on a throne."

On hearing this, the King grasped his beard and laughed heartily. "Easily done," he cried. "The task is to stay there."

With his own hand he led the old soldier to the throne, placed his usual crown upon his head, the royal sceptre in his hand, and with a gesture presented him to all assembled there. There sat the old soldier, with his war-worn face, great bony hands and lean shanks, smiling under the jewelled crown at the company. A merry scene it was.

Then the King earnestly asked the old soldier if he had anything in mind for the future, whereby he might show him his favour. Almost as if by magic, it seemed, the memory of the beldame in the forest came back into the old soldier's head, and he said: "Well, truth's truth, your Majesty, and if there *was* such a thing in my mind, it was pigs."

"Pigs!" cried the King. "So be it, and so be it, and so be it! Pigs you shall have in plenty," said he. "And by the walls of Jerusalem, of all the animals on God's earth there's none better—fresh, smoked, or salted."

"Ay, sir," said the old soldier, "and even better still with their plump-chapped noddles still on their shoulders and the breath of life in their bodies!"

Then the King sent for his Lord Steward and bade that seven changes of raiment should be prepared for the old soldier, and two mules saddled and bridled, and a fat purse of money put in his hand. Besides these, the King commanded that out of the countless multitude of the royal pigs should be chosen threescore of the comeliest, liveliest and best, with two lads for their charge.

And when towards sundown a day or two after the old soldier set out from the Royal House into the forest with his laden mules, his pigs and his pig-lads, besides the gifts that had been bestowed on him by the twelve noble young Princes and Princesses, he was a glad man indeed. But most he prized a worn-out gold and silver slipper which he had asked of the youngest Princess for a keepsake. This he kept in his knapsack with his magic scrap of root and other such treasures, as if for a charm.

Little Red Riding Hood

In the old days when countrywomen wore riding-hoods to keep themselves warm and dry as they rode to market, there was a child living in a little village near the Low Forest who was very vain. She was so vain she couldn't even pass a puddle without peeping down into it at her apple cheeks and yellow hair. She could be happy for hours together with nothing but a comb and a glass; and then would sit at the window for people to see her. Nothing pleased her better than fine clothes, and when she was seven, having seen a strange woman riding by on horseback, she suddenly had a violent longing for just such a riding-hood as hers, and that was of a scarlet cloth with strings.

After this, she gave her mother no peace, but begged and pestered her continually, and flew into a passion or sulked when she said no. When, then, one day a pedlar came to the village, and among the rest of his wares showed her mother a strip of scarlet cloth which he could sell cheap, partly to please the child and partly to get a little quiet, she bought a few yards of this cloth and her-self cut out and stitched up a hood of the usual shape and fashion, but of midget size and with ribbons for strings.

When the child saw it she almost choked with delight

and peacocked about in it whenever she had the chance. So she grew vainer than ever, and the neighbours became so used to seeing her wearing it in all weathers, her yellow curls dangling on her cheeks and her bright blue eyes looking out from under its hood, that they called her Little Red Riding-Hood.

Now, one fine sunny morning her mother called Little Red Riding-Hood in from her playing and said to her: "Now listen. I've just had news that your poor old Grannie is lying ill in bed and can't stir hand or foot; so as I can't go to see her myself, I want *you* to go instead, and to take her a little present. It's a good long step to Grannie's, mind; but if you don't loiter on the way there'll be plenty of time to be there and back before dark, and to stay a bit with Grannie, too. But *mind*, go straight there and come straight back, and be sure not to speak to anybody whatsoever you meet in the forest. It doesn't look to me like rain, so you can wear your new hood. Poor Grannie will hardly know you!"

Nothing in this long speech pleased Red Riding-Hood so much as the end of it. She ran off at once, and as she combed her hair and put on her hood, she talked to herself in the glass. There was one thing: Red Riding-Hood liked her Grannie pretty well, but she liked the goodies her Grannie gave her even better. So she thought to herself: "If the basket is heavy, I shall take a little rest on the way; and as Grannie's in bed, I shall have plenty to eat when I get there because I can help myself, and I can bring something home in the empty basket. Grannie would like that. Then I can skip along as I please."

Meanwhile, her mother was packing up the basket— a dozen brown hen's eggs, a jar of honey, a pound of butter, a bottle of elderberry wine, and a screw of snuff. After a last look at herself in a polished stew-pan, Red

Riding-Hood took the basket on her arm and kissed her mother goodbye.

"Now, mind," said her mother yet again, "be sure not to lag or loiter in the Low Forest, picking flowers or chasing the butterflies, and don't speak to any stranger there, not even though he looks as if butter wouldn't melt in his mouth. Do all you can for Grannie, and come straight home."

Red Riding-Hood started off, so pleased with herself and with her head so packed up with greedy thoughts of what she would have to eat at the end of her journey that she forgot to wave back a last goodbye before the path across the buttercup meadow dipped down towards the woods and her mother was out of sight.

On through the sunny lanes among the butterflies she went. The hawthorns, snow-white and crimson, were in fullest flower, and the air was laden with their smell. All the trees of the wood, indeed, were rejoicing in their new green coats, and there was such a medley and concourse of birds singing that their notes sounded like drops of water falling into a fountain.

When Red Riding-Hood heard this shrill sweet warbling she thought to herself: "They are looking at *me* as I go along all by myself with my basket in my bright red hood." And she skipped on more gaily than ever.

But the basket grew heavier and heavier the further she journeyed, and when at last she came to the Low Forest the shade there was so cool and so many strange flowers were blooming in its glens and dingles, that she forgot everything her mother had told her and sat down to rest. Moss, wild thyme and violets grew on that bank, and presently she fell asleep.

In her sleep she dreamed a voice was calling to her from very far away. It was a queer husky voice, and

seemed to be coming from some dark dismal place where the speaker was hiding.

At sound of this voice calling and calling her ever more faintly, she suddenly awoke, and there, not more than a few yards away, stood a Wolf, and he was steadily looking at her. At first she was so frightened she could hardly breathe, and could only stare back at him.

But the moment the Wolf saw that she was awake he smiled at her, or rather his jaws opened and he grinned; and then in tones as wheedling and butter-smooth as his tongue could manage he said: "Good-afternoon, my dear. I hope you are refreshed after your little nap. But what, may I ask, are *you* doing here, all alone in the forest, and in that beautiful bright red hood, too?" As he uttered these words he went on grinning at her in so friendly a fashion that little Red Riding-Hood could not but smile at him in return.

She told him she was on her way to her Grannie's.

"I see," said the Wolf, not knowing that through his very wiliness he would be stretched out that evening as cold as mutton! "And what might you have in that heavy basket, my dear?"

Little Red Riding-Hood tossed her head so that her curls glinted in a sunbeam that was twinkling through the leaves of the tree beneath which she was sitting, and she said, "My Grannie is very very ill in bed. Perhaps she'll die. So that's why I'm carrying this heavy basket. It's got eggs and butter, and honey and wine, and snuff inside it. And I'm all by myself!"

"My!" said the Wolf. "All by yourself; and a packet of snuff, too! But how, my little dear, will you be able to get in at the door if your Grannie is ill in bed? How will you manage that?"

"Oh," said Red Riding-Hood, "that will be quite easy.

I shall just tap seven times and say, 'It's me, Grannie'; then Grannie will know who it is and tell me how to get in."

"But how clever!" said the Wolf. "And where does your poor dear Grannie live? And which way are *you* going?"

Little Red Riding-Hood told him: then he stopped grinning and looked away. "I was just thinking, my dear," he went on softly, "how very lucky it was we met! I know your Grannie's cottage well. Many's the time I've seen her sitting there at her window. But I can tell you a much, *much* shorter way to it. If you go *your* way, I'm afraid you won't be home till long after dark, and that would never do. For sometimes one meets queer people in the Low Forest, not at all what you would care for."

But what this crafty wretch told her was a way which was at least half a mile further round. Red Riding-Hood thanked him, seeing no harm in his sly grinning, and started off by the way he had said. But he himself went louping off by a much shorter cut, and came to her grandmother's cottage long before she did. And there was not a living thing in sight.

Having entered the porch, the Wolf lifted his paw and, keeping his claws well in, rapped seven times on the door.

An old quavering voice called, "Who's there?"

And the Wolf, muffling his tones, said, "It's me, Grannie!"

"Stand on the stone, pull the string, and the door will come open," said the old woman.

So the Wolf got up on to his hind legs and with his teeth tugged at the string. The door came open, and in he went; and that (for a while) was the end of Grannie.

But what Master Wolf had planned for his supper that

evening was not just Grannie, but Grannie *first* and then
—for a titbit—Red Riding-Hood afterwards.

And he knew well there were woodmen in the forest,
and that it would be far safer to wait in hiding for her
in the cottage than to carry her off openly.

So, having drawn close the curtains at the window, he
put on the old woman's clean nightgown which was
lying upon a chair, tied her nightcap over his ears,
scrambled into her bed, drew up the clothes over him,
and laid himself down at all his long length with his head
on the pillow. There then he lay, waiting for Red Riding-
Hood and thinking he was safe as safe; and an ugly heap
he looked.

All this time Red Riding-Hood had been still loitering,
picking wild flowers and chasing the bright-winged
butterflies, and once she had sat down and helped herself
to a taste or two of her Grannie's honey.

But at last her footsteps sounded on the cobbles; and
there came seven taps at the door.

Then the Wolf, smiling to himself and mimicking the
old woman, and trying to say the words as she had said
them, called, "Who's there?"

Red Riding-Hood said, "It's me, Grannie!"

And the Wolf said, "Stand on the stone, pull the string,
and the door will come open."

Red Riding-Hood stood on her tiptoes, pulled the
string, and went in; and one narrow beam of sunshine
strayed in after her, for she left the door a little ajar. And
there was her Grannie, as she supposed, lying ill in bed.
The Wolf peered out at her from under the old woman's
nightcap, but the light was so dim in the cottage that at
first Red Riding-Hood could not see him at all clearly,
only the frilled nightcap and the long, bony hump of him
sticking up under the bedclothes.

"Look what *I've* brought you, Grannie," she said. "Some butter, a jar of honey, some eggs, a bottle of wine, and a packet of snuff. And I've come all the way by myself in my new red riding-hood!"

The Wolf said, "Umph!"

Red Riding-Hood peeped about her. "I ex*pect*, Grannie," she said, "if I was to look in that cupboard over there, there'd be some of those jam-tarts you made for me last time I came, and some cake too, I ex*pect*, to take home, Grannie; and please may I have a drink of milk *now?*"

The Wolf said, "Umph!"

Then Red Riding-Hood went a little nearer to look at her Grannie in bed. She looked a long, long time, and at last she said, "Oh, Grannie, what very bright eyes you have!"

And the Wolf said, "All the better to *see* with, my dear."

Then Red Riding-Hood said, "And oh, Grannie, what long pointed nails you have!"

And the Wolf said, "All the better to *scratch* with, my dear."

Then Red Riding-Hood said, "And what high hairy sticking-up ears you have, Grannie!"

"All the better to *hear* with, my dear," said the Wolf.

"And, oh, Grannie," cried Red Riding-Hood, "what great huge big teeth you have!"

"All the better to *eat* with!" yelled the Wolf, and with that he leapt out of bed in his long nightgown, and before she could say "Oh!" Little Red Riding-Hood was gobbled up, nose, toes, hood, snuff, butter, honey and all.

Nevertheless, that cunning greedy crafty old Wolf had not been quite cunning enough. He had bolted down such a meal that the old glutton at once went off to sleep on the bed, with his ears sticking out of his nightcap, and his tail lolling out under the quilt. And he had forgotten to shut the door.

Early that evening a woodman, coming home with his axe and a faggot when the first stars were beginning to shine, looked in at the open cottage door, and instead of the old woman saw the Wolf lying there on the bed. He knew the villain at sight.

"Oho! you old ruffian," he cried softly, "is it *you*?"

At this far-away strange sound in his dreams, the Wolf opened—though by scarcely more than a hair's breadth —his dull, drowsy eyes. But at glimpse of the woodman, his wits came instantly back to him, and he knew his danger. Too late! Before even, clogged up in Grannie's nightgown, he could gather his legs together to spring out of bed, the woodman with one mighty stroke of his axe had finished him off.

And as the woodman stooped over him to make sure, he fancied he heard muffled voices squeaking in the wolf's inside as if calling for help. He listened, then at once cut him open, and out came Red Riding-Hood, and out at last crept her poor old Grannie. And though the first thing Red Riding-Hood did, when she could get her breath again, was to run off to the looking-glass and comb out her yellow curls and uncrumple her hood, she never afterwards forgot what a wolf looked like, and never afterwards loitered in the Low Forest.

As for her poor old Grannie, though that one hour's warmth and squeezing had worked wonders with her rheumatism, she lived only for twenty years after. But then, it was on the old woman's seventieth birthday that Red Riding-Hood had set out with her basket.

It was a piece of rare good fortune for them both, at any rate, first, that the woodman had looked in at the cottage door in the very nick of time; next, that he had his axe; and last, that this Wolf was such a senseless old glutton that he never really enjoyed a meal, but swallowed everything whole. Else, Red Riding-Hood and her Grannie would certainly not have come out of him alive, and the people in the village would have had to bury the wicked old rascal in the churchyard—where he would have been far from welcome.

Jack and the Beanstalk

———————◄○●○►———————

There was once a boy named Jack, and he lived with his mother who was a widow. All they possessed was one old cow. What was worse, it looked as if they would never have anything else, for Jack, although he had his good points, was idle. At least, he wasn't exactly idle; but he hated doing what he didn't *like* doing —and that was most things. One thing he delighted in, though, and that was to think and dream of what he would do in the future: of how he would go off on his travels and see the world, and make his fortune, and then come back to his mother, and they would live happily ever after.

But far from coming back to his mother, she would hardly let him out of her sight. So he mooned and moped, and at last they were so poor there was scarcely a crust in the larder, and there was nothing for it but to sell their old cow.

Jack's mother hated the thought of parting with their cow. She had been a good friend to them for many a year. But since there was no help for it, she told Jack over and over again to be sure to get a good price for her.

"Mind you, Jack," she said, "they'll cheat you if they can. They've got tongues like serpents. But if you can't do no better, bring the old beast home again, and we'll all starve together."

Jack told his mother not to worry. He said he knew "all about that", and could give as good as he got; then, having cut himself a hazel switch and kissed her goodbye, he set off.

It was still early, and a fine, bright morning, with dew on the grass, and Jack felt in very good spirits as he went whistling on his way. But the nearest market town was a good many miles off, and as the day wore on and the sun edged higher, the lanes between their high banks became hot and dusty, and Jack soon grew tired of trudging along as if the only thing in the world worth following was an old cow's tail. So he began to take things easy. Once he stopped to lie down to get a drink of water at a little wayside spring, and every now and again he sat for a bit on a gate or a stile, leaving the cow to browse the grass in the hedge, while he looked at whatever there was to see—which was plenty, for it was the time between spring and summer.

Still, Jack was pretty tired of his journey when, about eleven o'clock, he met a man coming along. This man was a middle-sized man, but rather stout; he had little bright blue eyes in his round face, and a smile all over it.

"Good-morning, son," says he to Jack, looking first at him and then at the cow; "and what might you be after this fine morning?"

" 'Might!' " said Jack, pushing back his cap and mopping his hair. "What *I*'ve been after all the morning is this old cow."

"And what," said the man, "is the old cow after?"

"She's after being sold," said Jack, "because me and my mother want the money, and we can't keep her any more."

"And what," said the man, still looking at Jack, "what d'ye think she'll fetch?"

"There's not a better cow than that cow for miles around," said Jack, "and I ought to know, for we've had her for years and years."

The stranger laughed, and glanced again at Jack as if he liked the look of him. "No question, son," he said, "but you know how many beans make five."

"Ay," said Jack with a grin, "two in each hand and one in your mouth."

"Why, so!" said the stranger. "And talking of beans, here you are!" With that he suddenly drew out of his breeches pocket a small handful of bean-seeds. "What d'ye say to *them*?" he said. "And look well, son, for these here aren't no ordinary beans, but magic beans; and once had, you'll never want for more." His little blue eyes shone like bits of china as he looked at Jack.

Jack stared hard at the beans; and partly because of what the man had said and partly because of what they looked like, he had never set eyes on anything he wanted worse. They were not only more than twice the size of any bean-seeds he had ever seen and of a marvellous clear colour, but there was a look and appearance to them past describing; as though, in spite of lying so still and smooth in the man's hand—like smooth, water-worn, kidney-shaped pebbles from far down out of the deep blue sea—they were cramful of life and (which was just what the man had said) magic.

Jack turned his eyes away a moment, and thought of what his mother had said, then he glanced at the old cow munching the wayside weeds, then he looked at the man again with his open smiling red face, and last his eyes fixed themselves once more on the beans.

"How many of 'em will you give me," he said in a husky voice, "if—if they be what you say they be?"

"Seven," said the man.

Jack licked his lips. "And what'll I do with them?" he asked still more huskily.

"Answering *that*," said the man, "why, being magic, it's not what you'll do with them that matters, it's what they'll do with themselves."

Jack's eyes seemed to twirl completely round in his head. "Right," he said, "seven!"

So the man counted out the seven beans into Jack's palm, picking out the brightest colours and the best shapes, then, with a last solemn, friendly wink, he himself turned one way with the old cow, and Jack turned back and went off the other.

Even though he stopped every now and again to look at his beans, and, with a little spit, to polish one or two of them on his sleeve, Jack came in sight of home in about half the time he had taken until he met the stranger; but now he went more slowly. He had hardly put his hand on the latch of the garden gate when his mother caught sight of him over her washtub from the window and ran out.

"Bless *me*, Jack!" says she, "you *have* been quick; and me scarcely able to breathe thinking of you and all. How much?"

Jack stood very still, and all of a sudden the blood seemed to trickle out of his body, and his beans seemed to be of no more value than bits of flint in the road.

"Well, mother, I went on and on," he began, "and just before I got to the old bridge, I see a man coming along. He was a fat man, and as he came along his face——"

"Yes?" said his mother.

"Well," Jack continued, the words coming slower and slower, "this man—he looked at the cow and he looked at me, and he asked me what I was after, and I told him;

and then he said, what was the old cow after, and I told him; and then——"

"Mercy on us!" cried his mother; "if you don't tell me how much this very minute, I shall drop down dead where I stand."

"He give me these, mother," said Jack, fetching out the beans from his breeches pocket, and holding them out in his clammy palm. "At least, there are seven; and he—he said they were magic, mother——"

Jack's mother stared at the beans; her face had suddenly gone white as chalk, and she seemed to be trembling all over.

"Them!" she said. "Them! Oh, Jack!" She could say no more. With fingers still wet and cockled from the washtub, she caught Jack's outstretched hand such a slap that the beans were scattered in all directions; and then she suddenly burst out crying and ran off into the house.

Jack hid himself for the rest of the afternoon, never going near the house until dusk, then, having crept in and found an old crust in the larder, he had a drink of water and went off to bed.

Strange dreams he had; but the strangest of all was to come in the morning after he had woken. For when, first thing, he opened his eyes, his room was full of a dim greenish twilight; and though the birds were all merrily singing their morning chorus, it looked almost as dark as night at his lattice window. It was as though the cottage lay in a dense shadow. He pushed open the window and looked out, and, sure enough, it was no wonder the house had seemed to be in shadow, for he could see nothing but a tangle of green stalks or bines and leaves—stalks as thick as rope, and leaves a foot long at least, and with sprays of buds like cherries already showing. This great tangle of growth had its roots right under his window, but though he leaned over the narrow sill so far that he nearly toppled out, he couldn't catch any glimpse of the top of it.

How Jack got into his shirt and breeches that morning he didn't know. His head was all of a whirl; but almost before you could say Jack Robinson he found himself, shoes in hand, creeping down the narrow staircase, not daring even to breathe. But even when he got out into the garden and had come close up under the huge beanstalk, he couldn't see to the top of it. It wreathed and reared itself up and up and up above his head till its fresh green twinings vanished into the uttermost blue of the sky.

Jack's heart was thumping like a steam engine. Then the man hadn't cheated him! The beans *were* magic! Yes, and had mounted up from earth to heaven in the dark of but one brief night. Now the sun was beginning to rise in the east—as though out of a huge furnace; the morning breeze whistled softly in the twisted stems of the beanstalk; birds were fluttering about it, as if in curiosity and wonder, and a skylark was shrilling, circling up and up.

Jack could bear himself no longer. He gave a last long look at his mother's window. Her curtains were drawn, she was still asleep. Indeed, he seemed to be the only human being stirring yet, and almost before he knew it, he had started to climb the beanstalk. He climbed and climbed and he climbed and he climbed, every now and then pausing to take breath and to look down on the scene he had left behind him. Far, far below through the air, and no bigger than a rabbit-hutch, he could see his mother's cottage, and behind it the green hill, and a little bit to the west of that the old square stone tower and glinting copper weathercock of the village church, but all so dwarfed and smalled in the distance that even the widest field in view, pale-green with young wheat, looked no bigger than a cotton handkerchief.

Soon he seemed to be at evens with the sun, its great ball like molten glass; still, on he went until he could almost peep over the very edge of the round tilted world into the blue of space, and his head went so dizzy he had to shut his eyes.

At last he reached the very tiptop of the beanstalk, for there it stopped. Jack stepped off, and found himself in a strange country indeed. It seemed to be another layer. It must, he thought, be hidden from the earth by the dazzling blue of the heavens. Anyhow, here he was, and glad to be so. It was a country of smooth open hills and verdant valleys, no fences, walls or hedges, with a low shallow sky over all, and not a single house or habitation to be seen, except in the distance where stood a huge, louring Castle.

Jack stood and looked about him, his heart still thumping away under his ribs, in part because of the long climb he had had, and in part because of the strangeness of this new country he was in. By this time he was famishing hungry, for he had had precious little supper and no breakfast, so he decided to set off at once to the Castle in hope to get something to eat and drink.

He had not gone above a mile or so when, close by a coppice of willows, he met a stranger, and this was a woman. She had a long, pale face under her mantle, and dark eyes looking almost as if she had come out of a dream, and she asked Jack where he was bound for. Jack told her, to the Castle.

"Then go with care, Jack," she said, naming his name, "for in that Castle lives an Ogre. All his treasures have been stolen. Keep your wits, then, Jack, when he comes near; and creep soft as a shadow. It's danger. But having come, go on; and remember my bidding."

Jack thanked this stranger and went on, but when in a little while he ventured to look back after her, she was gone. That word *ogre* stayed in his mind, and he began to wonder why there were no signs of human beings to be seen at all—no houses, or fields even; and it was so utterly silent that even the rattle of a stone under Jack's shoes startled him as though a voice had called. There were a few trees, but no birds sang in them, though now and again sulphur-coloured butterflies were to be seen playing in the hollows over the blue-flowering heads of a tufty weed like hemp agrimony.

Once Jack heard, too, a sound like the clapping of tiny pebbles together, but this he thought was only insects. Still, he stayed for nothing, but trudged on; and the Castle came steadily nearer. Yet, even now, it was much further away than he had supposed, and by the time he reached the great gates in its towering walls it was getting towards evening. He craned back and gazed high above his head at the stone walls, and at thought of the Ogre his blood went cold in his body.

He stood there looking awhile, then knocked with his knuckles. No answer. He knocked again, then kicked with his shoe; but still no answer. Then, seeing a rusty and cobwebbed bell-pull hanging down in the corner, he tugged at that. A footstep sounded, and a narrow door cut out in one of the big spiked gates opened a little, and a woman looked out at him. Seeing only this boy, Jack, there, she gazed at him in astonishment, and asked him what he wanted.

Jack pulled at his cap and smiled at her as pleasantly as he could, and asked if he might have a bite of food and a mug of drink.

"And if you please, mum," he went on, pulling a long face, "it's getting on for night and bitter cold, and I've nowhere to sleep." He could speak as wheedling as a blind beggar when he liked, and the woman at this looked a good deal more friendly. Nevertheless, she shook her head at him, peered about her as if she were half-afraid of what she might see, and only warned him again and again to turn back.

"Run off as fast as ever you can," she said, "and go back to the place you've come from. Though where *that* is I can't so much as give a guess," she said. "What's more, boy, you have precious little time, for the Ogre that lives in this Castle may be back at any minute, and you're just the kind of morsel he'd be glad to see. Don't you mistake me, boy: he'd gobble you up before his supper quicker than a cat eats flies; so run off as fast as you can, and get out of sight and smell."

Jack tried his very utmost not to show how deadly frightened he felt at this. But having come so far, he thought to himself, it was no good turning back now, especially after what the stranger had said; so he smiled at the woman again, and begged and begged, if only for a drink of water.

"I'm that dry, mum, with walking," he said, "my tongue's like a chip of wood. And run away, mum! My legs would give under me!"

The woman continued to look at him through the little gate, and still she hesitated; but at last—and already the evening light was beginning to fade—she opened the door wider and beckoned him in. "Come along, then, quick," she said. "But I warn you, if the Ogre catches so much as a glim of you, you'll be gone for good and all."

"Yes, mum," said Jack as steadily as he could manage, and followed her in under the dark echoing stone arch and across a courtyard, then down a corkscrew flight of worn stone steps into the Ogre's kitchen, taking good care to remember exactly the way he went. This kitchen, with its square stone flags, prodigious stools and potboard, was almost as big as a small church, but cheerful, for the tea-tray plates on the dresser that seemed to be of pewter, twinkled merrily in the fire-shine.

Jack saw, too, where the Ogre's chair was drawn up to the table, but he could see nothing of what was *on* the table except the top of a metal pepper-pot like a flour dredger, because he was not tall enough. A thin smoke was floating up out of a crack in the brick oven, which seemed a mighty big oven even for a giant, and on a spit over the fire was what looked like a sheep roasting.

The woman sat him down on a log of wood so near the great stone fireplace that it was a little too warm to be comfortable. She gave him a hunch of bread and a mug of buttermilk. But the mug was so large and heavy that Jack could scarcely lift it to his mouth. However, he was famished for want of food, and he didn't much mind that; and while he munched he looked about him. There was plenty to see.

As he was sipping his buttermilk, there suddenly broke out a knocking in the back of the Castle, so loud that even the windows shook. At this the woman seemed to be a good deal put about. She hastily snatched away Jack's mug, scattered his crumbs with her apron, pushed Jack himself into a fusty cupboard near the hearth, and all but closed its door. Jack guessed pretty well why this had happened, so he sat there quiet as a mouse in the heat, keeping away from the wall nearest the fire, and listened.

As soon as the Ogre appeared at the door leading into the kitchen, he slowly lifted his head and began sniffing and snuffing about him in the air, then bawled out in a resounding voice:

" Fee, fi, fo, fum!
I smell the blood of an Englishman.
If he be living or if he be dead,
I'll grind his bones to make my bread."

Jack, keeping well back and peeping out of the cupboard, at sound of this roaring voice fairly shook in his shoes.

"Peace, peace!" said the dark woman to the giant. "You weary me with your silly shouting. Where are your wits? What you smell must be the two travellers that lie in the dungeon. And you know yourself they're not ready yet."

The Ogre mumbled and grumbled, and never ceased doing so until the woman had somehow lugged the great roast off the spit on to a dish, and he had sharpened his knife and begun his supper. There was a platter of red marrow-bones, too, which he crunched up like brandy-balls.

When he had eaten and drunken—and a mighty ugly noise he made over it—he roared at the woman to bring him his money-bags, and a hard job she had to carry them. There were twenty-two of these bags in all, containing pieces of gold and silver almost of the size of plates and saucers. Jack's mouth fairly watered as he watched, and he could scarcely keep from laughing at the Ogre's clumsiness and stupidity, for when he dropped a piece of money and it fell on the flagstones, he heard the ring of it and stooped to pick it up. But if the piece of money fell soundlessly on the mat of sheepskins at his feet, he paid no heed and left it lying there. Jack watched these pieces of money in particular.

When at last the Ogre had finished counting his money and had tied up his bags again—and he handled every coin as if it were his heart's delight—he sat back in his chair, and after staring for some little time into the empty air he fell asleep. Soon he was snoring like a gale in a chimney. But to make sure surer Jack waited in the cupboard for some little time before even stirring. Then as quiet as a shadow, he crept out over the flagstones, and keeping well away from the Ogre's boots, he stuffed four or five of the smaller pieces of money into his jacket pockets, and tucked one or two of the larger (and all of gold) under his arm. Then he tiptoed out of the kitchen, up the stone steps, and out by the wicket gate. Once out, he set off as fast as he could for the Beanstalk.

Now and again he looked back or stayed to listen, but there was not a sound to be heard. The money was heavy, and it was dark in spite of the star-shine which shone like a faint luminous mist in the air, but he'd had a good meal, felt as happy as a skylark, and trudged on rejoicing.

His mother had been waiting up all night for him, and when she saw him come grinning in at the door, tears of sheer joy came into her eyes and splashed on to his cheeks. She hugged him in her arms and kissed him, and then pushed him away and scolded him for having put her in such a tremble!

But when Jack showed her his great gold pieces of money and told her his story and his adventures, and of the Ogre and his Castle, and all he had seen and done, she could scarcely speak for delight, and kissed him seven times over. Jack told her everything, began again, and then suddenly fell asleep in his chair, he was so tired out with it all. Without rousing him, his mother untied and took off his shoes, covered him up with a blanket and left him to have his sleep out.

After that all went easy for many a day. There was plenty to eat, Jack's mother bought herself a new bonnet and jacket, and a fine time they had together in the market town, coming home laden with parcels, besides what were sent by the carrier, while Jack's pockets bulged with more things he fancied than he had ever even dreamed of having his whole life long.

But though the days passed pleasantly enough, it was impossible for Jack to get the Beanstalk out of his head. It grew denser and greener every day, and now its flowers had begun to open. Even when he sat at his window making a boat out of a block of wood with his new knife, or spying at things through the enlarging glass he had bought, the fragrance of the beanflowers was always in the air, and as soon as the sun was that way their shadow was on the sill.

He longed beyond telling to be up on high again and to have just another peep at that strange, still, silent country. At last, one night as he lay in bed, he made up his mind that early the very next morning he would make another start, and perhaps climb only half-way, or having gone on to the top, merely take a look to see that the Ogre's Castle was still there, and wasn't a dream—even though it was perfectly certain the money was not!

This time, in case the woman of the Castle should know him again, he put on a different cap and jacket— an old blue cut-away jacket that his mother had bought from a sailor many years ago.

It was not yet six and a fine morning, though there was a thick heat-mist over the fields, when Jack began to climb the Beanstalk the second time. He climbed and he climbed and he climbed and he climbed until at last he stepped off and found himself yet again in the strange country of smooth-sloping hills and dark-green valleys. When late in the afternoon, but earlier than before, he reached the Castle and pulled at the rusty bell, the woman appeared as before at the little cut-out door and asked what he wanted.

A fine story he told her. But she answered again and again that she durst on no account let him in. Only a few weeks before, she told him, she had taken pity on a poor boy—and a boy much of the same looks and height as himself, though younger—who had come begging for food and lodging, and all the rascal had done in return for her kindness was to steal some of the Ogre's money and run away in the dark. But Jack persisted—still muffling and altering his voice and whining a little, as if he were dead-beat with his long journey—and entreated her so piteously that at last he persuaded her to let him in.

She gave him a good supper, too, and this time when the Ogre came home, hid him in the oven, for, there being only porridge and cold meat for the Ogre, there was scarcely more than a smoulder of fire left in the grate. The walls of the kitchen trembled at his tread. He seemed to be in a raging bad temper, too; the noise of him was like wagons rattling over cobblestones; and the instant he put his head in at the kitchen door he snuffed and snuffed and snuffed, and bawled:

> "Fee, fi, fo, fum!
> *I smell the blood of an Englishman.*
> *Be he living or be he dead,*
> *I'll grind his bones to make my bread.*"

"Tssh! Peace, peace!" said the woman. "You cry for a fleabite. It's nought but the ravens on the roof-top. They have fetched home a bit of tainted meat for their young." But it took some time to quiet him down.

When the Ogre had set to his dish of half-raw victuals and drunk his fill, he bade the woman bring him in his little Hen. Now this Hen was no common hen but a marvellous hen, and the Ogre seemed to have a particular fondness for the little creature. He smoothed her feathers

with his clumsy finger, and stooping down his head, pursed up his mouth to softly whistle to her, until to see his great face and the little Hen so close together, and this huge Ogre so endearing, was enough to make a cat laugh. He even began at last to whisper actual words to the little Hen, and Jack listened with all his ears.

"Henny-penny," began the Ogre——

> "*Henny-penny, henny-penny, henny-penny, hey!*
> *Cl'kk, cl'kk, cackle, cackle, lay, lay, lay!*"

At this the little Hen clucked and cackled, and cackled and clucked, and lo and behold, before a clock could tick a minute, in the platter of hay the Ogre had put ready for her she had laid an egg of solid gold. Jack peered out at the Hen, his eyes almost bolting out of his head. Yet she was but a little hen and not much bigger than a bantam, though her feathers shone like sunbeams in water, and her comb was redder than the finest coral, and her claws like old ivory.

"Ah," thought he to himself in the oven, "what wouldn't mother give for a sight of that!"

Presently the Ogre, having put the egg in his side pocket, with his great finger once more smoothed the plumage of the little Hen as she crouched in the hay, and then, sitting back in his chair, fell asleep, and was presently snoring so loud Jack could hardly hear himself think. This time (having swallowed the deepest breath of his life), Jack stepped even more softly and cautiously than before out of the oven, and across the flagstones. He had to climb on to a three-legged stool, too, to reach the table. Then he snatched up the little Hen, clapped her tight under his arm, and away he went.

The Hen squawked as loud as her small tongue would let her, but by good luck the Ogre's snoring drowned her cries, and Jack, having taken things easy the last mile or two—even stopping to rest for an hour or so at the foot of one of the low green hills in the first beams of sunrise —got safely down the Beanstalk a little before breakfast.

Even when he showed his mother the Hen—though she agreed it was the neatest, nattiest and sprightliest little hen she had ever seen—she could hardly believe Jack's story.

"Lor'! mother," said Jack at last, "you're just like a woman. I'd like to have seen *you* in the oven! But if you can't and don't and won't believe, then watch!" Stooping over the little Hen, he held out his finger above her tiny head and whispered as if in secret:

"Henny-penny, henny-penny, henny-penny, hey!
Cackle, cackle, cackle, cackle, lay, lay, lay!"

To his dismay, nothing whatever happened. He went cold all over. The little Hen merely looked at Jack with her beady red eye as if he were nothing more than a lumping boy in a jacket and breeches, with no more power over her than the old man in the moon.

His mother glanced at Jack, then at the Hen again. "It's all right, Jack," she said. "I think she's the nicest and wonderfullest little hen I've ever seen, and it don't matter about the eggs one single mite, it don't."

"Matter!" said Jack scornfully. "Peace, mother!" And he tried again, but this time the words came a little differently, and he whispered:

> "*Henny-penny, henny-penny, henny-penny, hey!*
> *Cl'kk, cl'kk, cackle, cackle, lay, lay, lay!*"

At *that* every gold-edged feather on the little Hen seemed to stir and shimmer; her eye gleamed like a carbuncle. She clucked and cackled, cackled and clucked, and lo and behold, in less than a minute Jack took out from beneath her gentle wings a tiny golden egg, about the size of a damson.

"There," said Jack, "what did I tell you, mother? That's solid gold."

Now, as Jack's mother took endless care of the little Hen, there was never any need at all for Jack to go off on his travels again. Yet—such was the way of him now—he simply couldn't be happy long at home, but pined for fresh adventures, thinking and dreaming night and day of the Castle and of the treasures he had seen in it, of the Ogre and the far silent country in which he lived.

So at last, one early morning, without saying a word to his mother, he started off again to climb the Beanstalk. He climbed and he climbed and he climbed and he climbed —and almost without pausing—until he reached the top and found himself again where he had longed to be.

This time, though he had once more dressed himself differently, in a dark pepper-and-salt jacket, trousers that had belonged to his father and been cut down, and a red neckerchief, he began to fear that the woman would never be persuaded to let him in. He begged and pleaded and implored. He squeezed his knuckles into his eyes, as he stood crouching and shivering under the bell-pull, to make the tears come.

"Not once, but twice," she kept telling him, "and within the last two months I took pity on just such a ragamuffin as you who came here begging for food. And with just such a way with him too—thieving rascal! But never again. The first went off with a bag of the Ogre's money, and the last stole his little magic Hen. If he sets eyes on him he'll skin him alive, and if another such viper cringes his way into this Castle, I shall never see morning again."

At this Jack stopped his whimpering, gave a sort of groan, and turned away. "Well, all I can say, mum," he said, "is this: that if that old Ogre is such a cruel wicked wretch as to lay hands on a beautiful lady like you, he deserves to be boiled, he does. It's *my* belief, mum, he eat up them two poor hungry boys you're speaking of and his chicken too, and didn't like to say so, so went and told a lie. Thank you, mum, but after what you've been telling me, I'd rather sleep in a ditch, I would, than go in there, and p'raps I shan't mind *anything* by morning."

At this the woman twisted quite the other way about. She assured Jack she hadn't meant to blame him for what the other wicked boys had done; and maybe the Ogre *had* made a mistake. And though Jack still pretended he was frightened to death at the thought of setting foot within her gates, she put her hand kindly on his shoulder, entreated him not to shiver and shake any more, and simply compelled him to follow her down the stone steps into the kitchen.

It was hot supper to-night, and an immense tortoise-shell cat lay in the fire-corner in a bushel basket when Jack sat down on his log, but by good fortune she was asleep. The woman treated him as if he were a long-lost son. She gave him a basin of broth, a saucer of hot meat and a drink out of a little barrel, and promised him—as soon as the Ogre had gone to bed—one of her pillows to sleep on by the fire. So Jack was feeling more comfortable outside and in when the Ogre himself came home again, though the sound of him was like a storm coming up out of the east.

This time the woman hid Jack in the copper, with the lid nearly all over him; and yet the moment the Ogre put his nose inside the kitchen door, he snuffed about him like a dog after a rabbit, and roared:

> "Fee, fi, fo, fum!
> *I smell the blood of an Englishman.*
> *Be he living or be he dead,*
> *I'll grind his bones to make my bread.*"

He was so hungry and in so evil a temper, that, in spite of all the woman could say—that the cat had just caught a mouse, that her needle had pricked her thumb, that there were fresh pig bones in the larder—he wouldn't be pacified, and with his huge club in his hand began to rummage round searching and searching for what he had sniffed out. Luckily for Jack, though the Ogre looked everywhere else, even into the great green soup tureen, the wood box, and his old top-boots, he forgot the copper.

At last, in a worse temper than ever, he sat down to his supper, and swilled and gourmandized as he had never swilled before. Two whole dishes of his half-cooked meat he golloped up before he was satisfied. At that rate, Jack reckoned, the old glutton must finish off a flock of sheep in less than a fortnight.

When the Ogre had finished he sighed and seemed better, and sat smiling, like a mummy, then told the woman to bring him his Harp. Jack heard the woman go out of the kitchen and come back, but before even, it seemed, the Ogre could have had time to lay a finger upon it, so marvellous clear and enchanting a music welled up between the stone walls of the kitchen—a music of scarcely more sound yet sweeter than water gurgling over ice or of birds warbling in the mountain-tops—that Jack (crouched up in the copper) couldn't help lifting his head for an instant above its rim just to see what the Harp looked like. Yet, though this music was like none he had ever even in sleep heard before, the Harp in size was less than half that of any ordinary harp, and seemed to be made only of wood and wires and catgut. But what amazed Jack most was that the Ogre was not so much as looking at its strings. The Harp's music welled up solely of itself. Jack bobbed his head down again, but never in all his life had he wished for anything so much as for this Ogre's Harp.

When at last the Ogre had wearied of its discoursing, he silenced the Harp by touching a little spring which Jack could not see, lay back, and soon, as of old, was fast asleep and snoring in his chair, his great head lolling and jerking to and fro on his shoulders, awful to behold. In due time, thinking his moment had come, Jack crept out of the copper, drew near the Ogre's chair, climbed up on to the three-legged stool, and, putting out his hand, gingerly lifted the Harp and turned to run off with it.

I it, as he might have guessed, at first touch of his fingers on its wood, its strings began to resound again, as if a spirit resided within it and were calling for help:

"Master! master! master! master!
The robber runs, but run thou faster!"

So shrill and sad and piercing were its notes that though
the Ogre's snoring was like the yowling and growling of
a hundred hungry dragons, it woke him instantly in his
chair.

At sight of him Jack was off like a knife. But the Ogre
had caught a vanishing glimpse of him in the doorway,
and with a bellow of rage came trundling after him.
Away went Jack, away went the Ogre; out of the kitchen, up the steps, out through the Castle gateway and
into the night. Lucky it was for Jack there was a fleece of
cloud over the sky, particularly as this night, the moon
was shining. A thin ground-mist, too, had risen in the

valleys, which hid him at times as first he dodged this way and next he dodged that. But still the Ogre came after him, with his club up ready and yelling as he ran.

Jack ran twice as fast that night as he had ever run in his life before, but still clutching tight hold of the magic Harp. And, what with the fleecy gleam of the moonlight up above and the music of the harp-strings and the roaring and bellowing of the Ogre down below, it was as if he were running in an unbelievable nightmare among a thousand silver waterfalls.

Indeed, if at last by good chance he had not pressed the secret spring of the magic Harp and so stopped its music (which up till then the Ogre could hear even when Jack himself was out of sight), and if the Ogre had not devoured such a prodigious supper and been less fuddled with sleep, he would certainly have caught Jack as easily as a cat a mouse.

Even as it was, he reached the top of the Beanstalk when Jack himself was not more than half-way down, and when Jack was rejoicing to think he had got safely away. But Jack soon realized his mistake; for suddenly the Beanstalk began to sway and tremble, as if in a whirlwind far above his head, and he could hear a breathing (for the Ogre had stopped yelling now) like the soughing of sea-water in a blowhole. He knew what *that* meant, and could scarcely cling on to the bines of the Beanstalk for sheer fright.

Having once looked up, indeed, and caught sight of the enormous great shoes of the Ogre descending one after the other like huge mill-stones over his head, he looked up no more. No monkey ever slipped down out of a tree in a forest so quick as Jack slipped down that Beanstalk; but still he held tight on to the magic Harp.

The very instant he got to ground, he rushed to the

woodshed, caught up an axe, doubled back to the Bean-stalk, and hacked and hacked and hacked and hacked. But only just in time. Down at last came the Beanstalk, down toppled the Ogre, and with such a thump his neck was broken there and then, and he never stirred more.

But it had been a near thing, and for a long time after-wards Jack was well content to stay quietly at home with his mother. Of summer evenings they would often sit together a little beyond the porch of the cottage, with its clump of jasmine, and when the stars began to blink in the heavens Jack would lay his hand softly on the wood of the Ogre's Harp. So sweet were its strains that even the little Hen, with her head tucked in beneath her gold-fringed feathers under the roof of her hutch, would cluck softly out of her dreams, as if in reply.

But, strangest thing of all, as thus the two of them, Jack and his mother, sat one evening—and this was some six months after the springing up of the Beanstalk—in the midst of this pining music there suddenly sounded out a hollow *Moo!* And what should they see gazing over the garden-hedge at them but their old cow come back—and with a garland of wild briony and traveller's joy twisted about its horns. Who could have entwined that garland—except the man Jack had met coming along the road that first fine morning—Nobody knows. But then, Nobody can't say.

The Turnip

O nce upon a time there were two brothers, or
rather half-brothers, for they had had the same
father, but different mothers; and no two human
beings could be more unlike one another.

The elder brother was as sly as a fox, and had no more
pity or compassion than a weasel. Almost as soon as he
could tell a groat from a rose noble, he had scrimped
together every bit of money he could get. As he grew up
he had always bought cheap and sold dear. He would
rub his hands together with joy to lend a poor neighbour
money, for he knew he was sure of getting ten times as
much paid back. Oh, he was a villain, and no mistake!

Yet he lived in a fine big house full of fine furniture,
with stone gateposts and a high wall all round his garden.
He dressed in a gown of velvet when he sat down to
supper, with two men in breeches behind his chair to
wait on him. There were never less than seven different
dishes on his supper table—all smoking hot; besides tarts,
jellies, and kickshaws. Up in a high gallery, all set about
with wax candles, stood fiddlers playing as fast as they
could with their bows on their fiddles, until he had
finished picking his bones and sopping up his gravy down
below.

Yet though this brother was so rich he had very few

real friends, and most of such people as might have been his friends hated him, chiefly because he was a mean and merciless greedyguts. The one thing he wanted was to rise in the world and have everybody else bow and scrape before him; and his one inmost hope was that some day the King would hear of him and of all his money, and invite him to come and dine with him at his Palace, and perhaps make him a nobleman. After that, he thought, he could die happy!

The other brother was as different from this as chalk from cheese. He had nothing more in the world than a meagre little farm of a few fields and meadows, three cows, a sow, a horse in stable too old to work, an ass a few years older, and his chickens, ducks and geese. He worked hard from early morning to night to keep even these. Yet he always seemed to be cheerful and never sick or sorry.

The only time he had ever asked his rich brother for help he got nothing but sneers and insults; and after that the servants set the dogs on to him. Yet he himself would never have turned even a hungry cur from his door—not, at least, if he had a bone in his cupboard. And rather than kill a mouse in a trap he'd carry it off half a mile from the farm to set it free, and then give his old brown house-cat an extra saucer of milk to make up for it.

Now one April evening, as this brother was feeding his poultry in the stackyard, and had just emptied his wooden bowl, suddenly, and as if out of nowhere, an old cross-eyed man popped up his head over the rough wall and asked him for a drink of water.

"Water!" said the farmer. "As much as you like, my friend—to drink, wash or swim in! But if you'll step inside, I can give you a taste of something with a little more flavour to it."

The Turnip

He led the old man kindly into the kitchen, and having cut him off a plate of good fat bacon and a slice or two of bread, he drew him a jug of cider and put that on the table. It was the best he could give, and the cross-eyed old man, though he ate little, and seemed not to be much accustomed either to sitting within four walls or to the taste of meat, thanked him heartily. And as he was about to go on his way he gave a squint at the sun, now low in the west, then another very quick and sharp at the farmer, and asked him if he grew turnips.

The farmer laughed, and said, Ay, he did grow turnips.

"There be some that grow turnips," mumbled the old man—and he had such a queer way of speaking his English you might have supposed he wasn't used to the tongue—"there be some," he mumbled, "that wouldn't spare even a blind man a cheese-rind; and there be some——" But here he stopped, and flinging up his hand into the air as if for a signal, he went on in a lingo which the farmer not only could not catch, but the like of which he had never heard before. Then the old man went away —out of the gate by the ash-tree and away. And the farmer thought no more of him.

One morning a month or two afterwards, the farmer went out to pull a turnip or two for his hot-pot, and noticed up in the north-west corner of his field what looked to be a green tufty bush growing where no sort of bush ought to be. He shaded his eyes with his hand and looked again—and was astonished. But as he drew nearer he saw his mistake, for what he had taken to be a bush was nothing else than what you would most expect in a turnip field—that is to say, a Turnip; but of a size and magnitude the like of which had never been seen in the world before, not even in the island where the people are all giants.

The Turnip

The farmer stood and marvelled. He couldn't take his eyes off this Turnip. He could scarcely believe his own senses; and it was some little time before he realized that what he was looking at was not only *a* Turnip, but was *his* Turnip. After that, he went off at once and called his neighbours to come. It took them all that day until evening to dig the Turnip out. Early next morning they brought a farm-wagon, and, after scraping off the earth on the root, and washing it down with buckets of water, they managed at last to heave and hoist it into the wagon. Then they rested a bit, to recover their breath.

The Turnip fitted the wagon as if it had been made for it. In colour it was like ivory shading off to a lively green at the crown, and to a deepening purple towards the base. Its huge tuft of leaves stood gently waving in the light of the morning sun like the feathers in the head-dress of a grand lady. They were as wide as palm-leaves, but a pleasanter green and prickly to the touch.

The next thing was to decide what to do with the Turnip. There was flesh enough in it to feed an army, and as for "tops", there were enough of them, as one of the farmer's old friends said, to keep a widow and nine children in green-meat for a hundred years on end.

"Oy," said another, "given they didn't rot!"

"Oy," said a third, "biled free!"

"Oy," said a fourth, "and a pinch of salt in the water."

And then they all said, "Oy."

But while his neighbours were talking the farmer was thinking, and while he was thinking he gazed steadily at his Turnip.

"What's in my *mind*, neighbours," he began at last, taking off his hat and scratching his head, "is that turnips is turnips, and of turnips as *such* I've got enough and to spare, which is nought but what anybody can see as looks around him. But that there monster is, as you might say, not the same thing nohow. That there is a Turnip which for folk like you and me is beyond all boiling, buttering, mashing, ingogitating and consummeration. And what's in my *mind*, friends—what's in my *mind* is whether you agree with me that maybe His Majesty the King would like to have a look at it?"

The question was not what the farmer's friends had expected. They looked at him, they looked at one another, and last they looked again at the Turnip—the fresh, rain-scented wind now blowing freely in its fronds.

Then altogether, and as if at a signal, they said, "Oy." The next thing was to get the Turnip to the Palace. It took two strapping cart-horses, as well as the farmer's ass harnessed up in front with a length of rope. But even at that, it needed a long pull and a strong pull and a pull altogether, with his neighbours one and all shoving hard on the spokes of the wheels, to get the wagon out of the field.

Once on the high-road, however, it rode easy, and away they went.

Long before the farmer neared the gates of the Palace the streets of the city were buzzing like a beehive. As, cart-whip in hand and leading his ass by the bridle, he slowly paced on his way, there was as much excitement as if he had fallen from the clouds. Everyone marvelled. But the people at the windows and on the housetops saw the Turnip best, for a good deal of the root was hidden by the sides and tailpiece of the wagon, and by the sacks laid over it.

When the wagon actually reached the Palace gates, it was surrounded by such a throng and press of people there was scarcely room to sneeze, but there the sentries on guard kept them all back, and the farmer led his ass and two horses into the quiet beyond, alone.

The Turnip

Not only did the King himself come out into the court-yard to see the Turnip, but he ordered that the tailpiece of the wagon should be let down, and a stool be brought out so that he could see it better. And much he marvelled at the Turnip. Well he might, for no mortal eye had ever seen the like of it before. He sent word to the Queen, too, and she herself with her ladies and all the royal family, down to the youngest, came out of the Palace to view and admire it, and the two small princes who were nine and seven were hoisted up by the farmer into the wagon itself beside the huge root, and the elder of them scrambled up and sat among the stalks and tops.

Not only was the King exceedingly amused at the sight of him (and not less so because the Queen was afraid the young rascal might have a fall); not only did he speak very graciously to the farmer, and himself from the bottom of his heart thank him for his gift; but he commanded that when the Turnip had been safely lifted down into one of his barns, the empty wagon should be loaded up with barrels of beer, a hogshead of wine and other dainties, and that this should be done while the farmer was taking refreshment, after his journey, in the royal pantry.

Nor was he in the least degree offended when the farmer begged that he might leave this awhile, so that he might himself help to remove the Turnip from the wagon, being very anxious that it should not come to the least harm.

Long after the farmer had gone home rejoicing, the King laughed out loud every time he thought of the Turnip and of his small son sitting up among its tops. Nor did he forget the farmer, but sent to enquire about him and to discover what kind of man he truly was. Nothing but good was told of him. So the King remem-

bered him with special favour, and of his grace bestowed upon him the place and quality of "Turnip Provider in Chief to the Whole of the Royal Family."

After that the farmer prospered indeed. The rich and wealthy for miles around (as they couldn't get his turnips) would eat no other radishes or carrots than his. He soon had the finest long-maned cart-horses in the kingdom, with cows and sheep in abundance, while his old mare and ass had a meadow all to themselves, with plenty of shade and a pond of fresh water fed by a brook. Nothing pleased him better than to give a great feast in his kitchen —and everybody welcome who cared to come. But search as he might among the company, he never again saw the squint-eyed old man who had spoken to him over the stackyard wall.

Now when his rich, covetous brother first heard of the Turnip and of the King's favours and graciousness to a creature he had always hated and despised, he was black with rage and envy for days together, and could neither eat nor sleep. It was not until he came to his senses again that he began to think.

"A Turnip! A Turnip!" he would keep on muttering. "To think all that came of a Turnip! Now if it had been a Peach, or a Nectarine, or a bunch of Muscatel Grapes! But a Turnip!"

Then suddenly a notion came into his head. He could scarcely breathe or see for a whole minute, it made him so giddy. Then he hastened out, got into his coach and went off to a certain rich city that was beyond the borders of his own country. There he sold nearly everything he possessed: his land, his jewels and gold plate, and most of his furniture. He even borrowed money on his fine house. Having by this means got all the cash he could, he went off to another street in the city where was the shop of a man who was a dealer in gems, and one celebrated in every country of the world.

There he bought the very largest ruby this man had to sell. It was clear and lustrous as crystal, red as pigeon's blood, and of the size of an Evesham plum, but round as a marble. The man, poising it in a sunbeam between his finger and thumb, said there had never been a ruby to compare with it. This is a ruby, he said, fit only for a King.

Nothing could have pleased his customer better, though when the man went on to tell him the price of the gem his very heart seemed to turn inside out. Indeed, there was only just enough money in the three money-bags which the jeweller's shopmen had carried in for him from the coach into the shop to pay for it. But he thanked the man, put the little square box carefully into an inside pocket, stepped briskly into his coach and returned home.

Next day, in his best clothes, he went to the Palace and asked the Officer at the entry if the King would of his grace spare him but one, or, at most, two moments of his inestimable time. The Chamberlain returned and replied politely that his royal master desired to know who his visitor *was*. The rich man was made very hot and uncomfortable by this question. For the first time in his life he discovered that he didn't know. He knew what he *had* (most of it was now packed into the ruby in his pocket). He knew what he thought of himself; but he didn't know what he *was*. It was no use telling the King's Chamberlain his name, since he felt sure the King had never heard of it; he might just as well say "Uzzywuzzy-bub", or "Oogoowoogy".

The only thing he could think to say—and it tasted as horrid as a black draught when he said it—was that when he was a child he had been allowed by his father to play with the boy who was now the farmer who had brought the King the Turnip—which was just as much the whole truth as the piggy of an orange is a whole orange.

When the King heard this he was so much amused that, sitting there in his Presence Chamber, he almost laughed aloud. He had guessed at once who his visitor was, for after enquiring about his beloved farmer (for beloved by everybody who knew him he truly was) he had heard much of this rich man—his half-brother. He knew what a mean skinflint he was, how he had robbed the poor and cheated the rich, and what kind of help he had given the farmer when he grievously needed it. And last, the King guessed well what he had now come for—to curry favour, and in hope of a reward. So he determined to teach this bad man a lesson.

When with his ruby he appeared trembling, bowing, cringing and ducking before him, the King smiled on him saying, that if he had known his visitor was a friend of the farmer who grew the Turnip, he would have been at once admitted into his presence.

The rich man, having swallowed this bitter pill as best he could, bowed low once more, his fat cheeks like mulberries.

The King then asked him his business. So, without more ado, the rich man fetched out of a secret pocket of his gown the casket which contained the great ruby, and with an obeisance to the very ground presented it to the King.

Now, though the farmer's Turnip, as turnips go, was such as no monarch in the world's history had ever seen before, this ruby, as Kings and rubies go, was not. But even if it had been, it would have made no difference to the King. To him it was not the gift that mattered, but the giver. Besides, he knew exactly why this rich man had come with his gem, and what he hoped to get out of it.

He smiled, he glanced graciously at the ruby, and said it was indeed a pretty thing. He then went on to tell his visitor that the prince, his small son, was not only fond of sitting on a farm wagon among the green tops of the biggest turnip there ever was, but also delighted in all kinds of coloured beads, stones, glass, marbles, crystals, and quartz and that his young eyes in particular would be overjoyed at sight of this new bauble. Then he raised his face, looked steadily at his visitor, and asked him what favour he could confer on him in return and as a mark of his bounty.

The rich man shivered all over with joy; he didn't know where to look; he opened his mouth like a fish, then, like a fish, shut it again. At last he managed to blurt out that even the very smallest thing the King might be pleased to bestow on him would fill him with endless rapture. For so he hoped to get ten times more than he would have dared to ask.

The King smiled again, and said that, since the rich man could not choose for himself, the only thing possible would be to send him something which he himself greatly valued. "Ay," said he, "beyond words."

The rich man returned to his half-empty house overjoyed at the success of his plan. He was so proud of himself and so scornful of the mean people in the streets and the shopkeepers at their doors, that wherever he looked he squinted and saw double. For the next two days he could hardly eat or sleep. He had only one thought, "What will His Majesty send me?"

He fancied a hundred things and coveted all. Every hour of daylight he sat watching at his window, and the moment he drowsed off in his chair at night, he woke at what he thought was the sound of wheels. As for the only servant he now had left, the poor creature was worn to a skeleton, and hadn't an instant's peace.

On the third morning, as the rich man sat watching, his heart all but ceased to beat. A scarlet trumpeter on a milk-white charger came galloping down the street. The rich man hastened out to meet him, and was told that a gift from the King was even now on its way. Sure enough, a few minutes afterwards there turned the corner an immense dray or wagon drawn by six of the royal piebald horses, with an outrider in the royal livery to each pair, while a multitude of the townsfolk followed after it huzzaing it on. Yet it approached so slowly that the rich man thought he would die of suspense. But when at last it reached his gates he hadn't long to linger. The great canvas covering of the wagon was drawn back, and there, on an enormous dish, lay the King's present, something, as he had said, that he valued beyond words. It was a large handsome slice of the farmer's Turnip.

At sight of it, at sight of the people, the rich man paused a moment—then ran. He simply took to his heels and ran, and if, poor soul, he had not been so much overfed and overfat, he might be running to this day.

The Wolf and the Fox

A foolish fox once made friends with a wolf. With his silky brush and pointed nose, he fancied himself a smart fellow, and hardly knew at first which way to look, he was so vain of his new company. But he soon found out that his fine friend was not in love with him for his own sweet sake, and that *being* a wolf, a wolf he was. For one thing, he was a villainous glutton and could never eat enough; and next, he had no manners.

"And what's for supper to-night?" he would say, with his white teeth glinting in the moon. "Bones! Bones! Lor', friend Fox, if you can't get me anything really worth eating, I shall soon have to eat *you*." It was an old joke now; and though he laughed as he said it, he did not look very pleasant when he laughed.

The fox grinned on one side of his face, but not on the other. "Well, friend Wolf," he said, "keep up your spirits. There's a farmyard over the hill where two plump young lambs are fattening. Softly now, and away we go!"

So off they went together. When they reached the farmyard the fox sneaked in through the gate, snatched up one of the lambs, leapt over the stone wall and carried it off to the wolf. After which, he trotted round to the henhouse to get his own supper in peace. But when the wolf had finished off his lamb—leaving not so much as a bone for his friend to pick—he felt hungrier than ever, and determined to slip away himself and get the other.

But he was so clumsy in scrabbling over the stone wall of the yard that the old mother sheep heard him, and began bleating aloud in the darkness. At this the farmer —who was sitting in his kitchen—ran out with his dog and a cudgel, and managed to give the wolf such a drubbing as he climbed back over the wall, that he came creeping back to the fox as wild with pain as he was with rage.

"A nice thing *you've* done," he said to the fox. "I went to fetch the other lamb, and I'm beaten to a jelly."

"Well," said the fox, "one's one and two's two; but enough is as good as a feast"; and he thought of the tasty young pullet he had stolen for his own supper.

Next day they decided to be getting off into the country where they were less well known. After a pleasant afternoon's journey, they found themselves on the edge of a little green coppice, and the wolf fell asleep in the sun. He woke up as surly as a bear with a sore head.

"Come, rouse, friend Fox! Supper!" he bawled. "What's for supper? No more lamb to-night. I'd sooner eat *you*!"

The fox trembled with rage, but he answered him civilly and said: "I seem to smell pancakes—rich pancakes. Squat here awhile, friend Wolf, and I'll see what can be done."

He slipped off and away to the other side of the wood, and came to a house from whose brick chimneys a faint smoke was going up laden with so sweet and savoury an odour of pancakes that the fox lifted his nose into the air and snuffed and snuffed again. Then first he crept this way; and then he crept that way; and at last he stole in through an open window, and so into the pantry, and leaping up on to a shelf, carried off at least six of the pancakes.

The wolf swallowed them down without so much as a thank'ee, and champed for more. The glutton then asked the fox which way he had gone. The fox told him. "You'll know the house by the smoke," he said, "and the window is by the water-butt. But step quiet, my friend, if go you must, for I heard voices." The greedy wolf, thinking that if the fox came with him to the house he would expect a share of the pancakes that were left, at once scuffled off alone into the night to finish the dish.

But he made such a hullabaloo in the pantry as he went sprawling along the shelf, upsetting a great cooking crock as he did so, that the farmer and his wife, and the friends who had been supping with them, heard his noise and came rushing in, and gave him such a basting that he hardly escaped with his life.

When he had licked his bruises and got some breath into his body again, he came snarling back to the fox, and blamed *him* for his beating. The fox coughed and turned his head aside; he could hardly speak for rage and contempt. However, the duck he himself had supped off was still sweet in memory; so he answered the wolf smoothly, reminding him that he had been given a fair warning. "Besides," said he, "as I've said before, enough is as good as a feast, friend Wolf; and with *some* sauces, much better."

Yet, even now, the wolf had not learnt his lesson. For, a very few evenings afterwards, though he could only limp along on three legs, and every bone in his body ached, he turned morosely on his friend the fox, and said: "Friend Fox, I'm sick and tired of you. You've no more wits than a rabbit. 'Sly,' indeed! Now, see here; if before that moon up there has climbed an inch in the sky you don't get me a meat meal, a tasty meal, and plenty of it— a supper worth a gentleman's eating, I'm saying—then it will surely be the last of you, for I'm *done* with your shilly-shallying."

The fox trembled and said, "Softly, softly, friend Wolf; why lose your temper? I do my best. This very morning I heard that the human that lives by the stream on the other side of the hill yonder has been killing a pig. A fat pig—a very fat pig; a pig *stuffed* with fatness. And the salt pork of that pig is packed in a barrel in the human's cellar. Ah, I see your mouth watering. Come, we will go together."

"Why, yes," said the wolf, "and you shall keep watch while I eat."

So the fox led him off by a green ride through the woods and over the crest of the hill, and by a cart-track, till they at last came down to a mill. It was a clear moon-shine night, with a touch of frost in the air. And as it chanced, there was a small, round-topped little door under the wall of the house that led into the cellar. The fox lifted its latch; paused; sniffed; listened; sniffed again.

His green eyes glistened like fireballs, as he turned his sharp muzzle and looked back at the wolf. "Come," he said, "and do not so much as grin or gruff, for the human of this house has a gun."

The wolf, being overfed and overfat, only just managed to scramble through the hole. But at last he followed the fox into the cellar, and was soon guzzling away at the barrel of salted pork.

"Tell me, friend Fox," he said, glancing over his shoulder, his jaws dripping, "why do you keep running to and fro? Restrain yourself. It pesters me. How can I feed in comfort with you fidgeting about? Keep still;

and you shall, perhaps, have a gobbet or two yourself. All depends on what I leave."

"Gobble on, gobble on," said the fox craftily. "There's plenty of time for me. But I warn you: don't make a noise, and don't eat too hearty!"

"Ah," said the wolf, "you thought this fine fat feast of pork was for you, did you? And after all my pains in finding it! Have no fear, my friend, there won't be much pork when *I've* finished."

At this, with a stroke of his paw and a shove of his shoulder, he turned the great salty tub clean over on the stones of the cellar; and a fine clatter it made.

Indeed, the miller, who was at that moment shaving himself in a looking-glass, hearing this noise in his cellar, supposed for a moment there was an earthquake. Then he snatched up his blunderbuss, and with the soapsuds still foaming on his cheek, came clumping down the stone steps.

The Wolf and the Fox

At first sound and sniff of him, the fox was out of the hole at a bound, and in a moment or two his friend the wolf was struggling hard to follow him. But the greedy guzzler had puffed and swilled himself out so fat with his feast of pork that, wriggle and wrench as he might, he could not squeeze through the hole. So there he stuck. And the miller, though he had lost a good half of his pork, at least gained a thick wolf's skin in exchange.

Meanwhile, the fox on the crest of the hill, hearing the roar of the blunderbuss, shivered a little, then danced a little dance all to himself in the moonlight. There and then he made up his mind that his next friend should not be one of the selfish and mighty ones, but of his own size and liking; and one with a brush.

The Three Sillies

———————————◦▶○◀◦———————————

There was once a farmer and his wife who had a daughter, and this daughter had a sweetheart, and a gentleman he was. Three days a week this gentleman used to come and see the daughter and stay to supper, and a little before supper time, the daughter used to go down into the cellar to draw the beer.

Now one evening, as the beer was running softly out of the barrel into the jug, she gave a great yawn, and in so doing looked up at the beams of the cellar over her head, and—stuck up there in one of them—she saw an old chopper. It was a broken old rusty chopper, and must have been sticking in the beam there for ages. But as she looked at the chopper—and the beer trickling softly on —she began to think and this is what she thought:

"Now supposing me and my gentleman up there get married soon, and we have a son we do, same as *my* mother and father had a daughter, and that son we have grows up and grows up, and keeps a-growing up, and when at last he's quite grown up he comes down here some evening, same as me here now as you might say, to draw the beer for supper, and that there old chopper comes *whopp* down on his head and chops off his head—my! what a dreadful, dreadful, *dreadful* thing it would be!" At this, she flopped down on the settle beside the cask, and burst out crying.

Now the farmer and his wife and the gentleman began to want their beer. So the mother went down after her daughter into the cellar, and found her sitting there on the settle beside the barrel, crying and crying, and the beer running out of the jug all over the cellar floor. So she asked her what was the matter.

And the daughter, sobbing and sobbing, said: "Oh, Mother, look at that old rusty chopper stuck up in the beam!" Her mother looked at the chopper.

"Now just you think, Mother," says she, "supposing now me and my gentleman up there was to get married soon, and we was to have a son, same as you and father had a daughter, which was me in a manner of speaking, and that son was to grow up, and up, and up, and one day he came stepping down into the cellar to draw beer, same as we are now, and that old chopper there stuck in the beam was to come *whopp* down and chop his head off, what a dreadful, dreadful, *dreadful* thing it would be!"

At this the farmer's wife, looking at the chopper, could contain herself no longer, but flopped down on the settle beside her daughter and burst out crying. So there sat the two of them. By-and-by the gentleman says to the farmer, "What about that beer?" So down came the farmer after his wife and his daughter and the beer; and there was the beer running all over the cellar floor.

"Why, whatever is the matter?" said the farmer.

The old wife told him just what the daughter had said. And when the farmer looked at the rusty chopper stuck in the beam, he could contain himself no more, and "Oh," said he, "what a dreadful, dreadful, *dreadful* thing it would be!" And down he squatted beside the other two on the settle, and burst out a-crying.

So at last the gentleman upstairs, being as dry as an oven, came down into the cellar to look for the farmer and the farmer's wife and their daughter and the beer; and there were these boobies, all three of them, sitting side by side on the settle, and crying and crying; and there was the beer trickling down all over the floor, and more of it out of the cask, by a long chalk, than in it. So

the gentleman first turned off the tap, then asked them what they were all sitting there crying for.

And "Oh," said they together, "look at that horrid old rusty chopper stuck in the beam. Supposing you were to have a son, and he grew up, and up, and up, and one evening, same as might be now, he came down here to draw beer and it fell down *whopp* on his head and chopped his head off, what a dreadful, dreadful, *dreadful* thing it would be!"

At this the gentleman burst out laughing. "Well," says he, "of all the sillies I ever set eyes on, you three are the silliest. That's just done for me! Off I go to-morrow morning, but I promise you this—if ever I find three sillies sillier than you three sillies, I'll come back there and then, and we'll have the wedding." So off he went.

Day after day the gentleman ambled along on his fat, red-roan mare, enjoying his travels, and at last he came to a cottage. It was an old cottage, and wallflowers were blowing in the garden, and very sweet too; and up there on the roof under its chimney were not only snapdragons and cat's valerian, but tufts of grass sprouting out of the thatch; and leaning against the thatch was a ladder. It was at *this* the gentleman stared, for the old woman of the cottage was doing her utmost to push her old cow up this ladder, but the cow wouldn't.

"Kem over!" she says. "Upadaisy!" she says; and there was the cow shooing and mooing and not daring to go.

The gentleman looking down from his horse said, "What's going on, dame?" The old woman told the gentleman that she was trying to get her cow up on to the roof so that she could eat the juicy tufts of fresh, green, beautiful grass up there under the chimney.

"Then when I have got her on to the roof," she said, "I shall tie the end of this here rope round her neck, and drop the other end down the chimney, and tie *that* end round my arm. So that way," she says, "I shall know if my old cow's safe on the roof or not."

"Well, well, well!" said the gentleman, and went on watching her. After a long time the old woman managed to do what she wanted, and there sat her cow on the thatch—all legs, horns, and tail—and a strange sight *she* was. But the moment the old woman had gone into the house, the poor old cow slipped on the thatch, and down she came, dangling by the rope round her neck, and was strangled. As for the old woman tied up to the rope by her arm inside the house, when the cow came down, up went she, and was jammed up inside the chimney and smothered in the soot.

Then of course the neighbours came running out; and the gentleman rode off on his horse; and as he went he thought to himself: "Well, of all the silly sillies that was *one*!"

He travelled on and on, and came one night to an inn. This inn happening to be full of company, there was only one way, the landlord told the gentleman, for him to sleep, and that was with a stranger in a great, double bed. So, as there was nothing better, he hung up his hat, went downstairs for some supper, came back, and after a bit of talking together he and the stranger were soon fast asleep in the great four-post bed.

When, about seven, the gentleman awoke in the morning, what should he see but that this stranger had hung up his breeches on to the two top knobs of the chest-of-drawers; and there he was, running to and fro, up the room and down again, trying might and main to *jump* into his breeches. First he got one leg in—that was no good. The next time he got the other leg in—that was no better. Sometimes neither leg went in, and that was worse. And he never got both. At last he stopped to take breath, and, mopping his head, said to the gentleman in the bed:

"My! You wouldn't believe it, but it takes me the best part of a solid hour every morning to get into those breeches of mine. How do you manage with yours?"

"Well, well, well!" said the gentleman, bursting out laughing. And he showed him.

As after breakfast he was mounting his horse—which the ostler had brought out of the stable—the gentleman suddenly thought of his bed-fellow and the breeches again, and burst out laughing. "Well, of silly sillies," he said to himself, "hang me if that wasn't a sillier silly still."

Off he went on his travels again, and at last came to a pretty village down Somerset way, with fine green trees in it and a pond. But quiet village it certainly was not, for all about this pond seemed to be collected the people for miles around, some with hayrakes, and some with brooms and besoms, and some with pitchforks; and there they were, all of them, raking and scrabbling, and scrabbling and raking in the water.

"Why," said the gentleman, "what's the matter?"

"Matter!" said they, "well you may ask it. Last night the old green moon tumbled into the pond, for old Gaffer Giles, coming home, looked in and saw her there, and we can't fetch her out nohow."

"Moon!" said the gentleman, bursting out laughing. "Wait till evening, my friends, and if she don't come swimming up into the East there, as right as ninepence, I'll eat my hat!"

But this only made them angry, and with their brooms and pitchforks and hayrakes they chased the gentleman and his horse out of the village.

"Well," said the gentleman to himself, as he rode off down the hill, "well, taking thirty or forty heads for one; they were the very worst silly I've ever seen."

So, true to his word, he turned back again, and a week or two after reached the farm and married the farmer's daughter. And that being so, maybe he was the silliest silly of all silly sillies. But who's to say?

Bluebeard

There was once a proud and foolish widow who had two daughters, Anne and Fatima. Anne was short and dark and plain; but she had a brave heart and sharp wits. Fatima was fair and slim, with long pale-gold hair; and all she thought of was fine clothes and dainty things to eat. And her mother's one hope and desire was that Fatima should get a rich husband.

"When Fatima is married," she would say to Anne, "we will look for a husband for you too. But that will be a far harder thing to manage. And I am sure you will not envy your sister even if you never get married at all."

Anne smiled to herself at this, for she thought, "If ever I marry, it's my husband will have done the 'looking'." But she held her tongue.

Now one day there came to this rich widow's house a stranger in a fine glass coach with four milk-white horses. The night was growing dark when he reached its gates, but he could see its high gateposts and the lights in its windows, and he sat looking at it a moment and stroking his beard. Then he sent a footman to the lady of the house, bidding him ask the way. At sight of the footman and the fine silver-lamped coach, the widow at once invited the stranger in.

He bowed low over her hand, thanked her a thousand

times, and explained that his coachman had lost his way and now night was down.

"He shall be punished, madam, all in good time," he said, looking at her as an old fat barn-door cock looks at a grain of barley. "But meanwhile would you be so kind as to tell me what road to take now, to the nearest inn?"

This silly widow, seeing his handsome clothes, and thinking what pleasant manners he had, for he bowed and smirked at every word he uttered, thought to herself, "Ah, here at last is the very husband I have been hoping for, for my dear dear Fatima."

There was but one thing about him that made her doubt a little. He had a long hooked nose between his little bright black eyes, and a blue beard. It was a blue beard so dark as to be almost black, and of the shape of a shovel, and he stroked it as he spoke to her—a strange beard! When he saw Fatima, he cast up his little eyes as if in astonishment at her beauty, and smiled and bowed again and kissed her hand. And the lady smiled, too. "Ah," she thought, "he has already fallen in love. And no wonder!"

The fair Fatima listened to his pretty speeches and drank in his flatteries as she sat beside him at supper, crumbling her bread and sipping her wine. And Bluebeard—for that was the name by which he was known to his neighbours —vowed to her mother that in his long life he had never set eyes on so fair and modest a damsel as her daughter, and the very next evening he asked for Fatima's hand in marriage. Her mother could scarcely contain herself for joy.

A few days afterwards—for Bluebeard said he must make no great stay from his own estate—there was a splendid wedding, with guests from far and near, and Anne was Fatima's bridesmaid. And after the wedding there was a Feast. There were fiddlers and trumpeters, and silver gilt dishes loaded with rich dainties and sweetmeats, and Bluebeard smirked and twiddled the great ring on his thumb, and the eating and drinking lasted till morning. The widow's only regret was that her two sons were not sharing in these joys, for they were away in foreign parts.

The next day Bluebeard led his bride to his coach; they waved their hands out of the window, and the coach rolled away. Besides the bags and chests full of Fatima's clothes in the cart that went with them, there was another great chest slung on to the back of the coach itself, and that held her dowry.

After some days' journey, for the huge heavy coach rolled on very slowly through the country ruts and rain, Bluebeard lifted his head and bade Fatima look out of the window. She did so, and on a little hill, rising above the green flat country round about it, she saw a vast dark mansion with turrets of stone.

"See, my dear, that is where you are going to live," he said. But though the house with its stone walls and turrets was a fine thing to look at, rising in solitude on its green hill, Fatima could not help but shiver, it looked so grim and forbidding. But she smiled at her husband, and he stroked his beard and watched the windows of the house as he drew near.

Now it seemed strange to Fatima that there was not a single soul to welcome them. But she soon found out that the country people hated Bluebeard, and refused even to sell him their butter and eggs and pigs and fowls, though to curry favour with them he had often tried to buy. When he came into sight the children ran and hid themselves, and every door was shut. Besides which, Bluebeard seemed to have no friends at all and not even a single visitor was ever seen at his gates. When she was alone—which was often—Fatima wondered why this should be. But she did not dare ask questions. For Bluebeard was often moody and silent, and she was sometimes so unhappy she wished she was home again.

Now one evening, as she was walking along the bank of a little river that looped its way through the green fields beneath the walls of Bluebeard's house on the hill, Fatima met an old woman gathering sticks. Fatima was feeling sad and doleful because she saw so little of her husband and because she was homesick; and though she had never done such a thing before, she stooped down and picked up one of the sticks that the old woman had dropped by chance out of her heavy faggot.

The old woman looked at her, muttered a blessing for her kindness, and then, after a swift searching glance at the house, whispered in her ear, "Where one is now, there once were many. Beware!"

But before Fatima could ask her what she meant by this queer secret saying, the old woman had hobbled off with her sticks.

A day or two after this, Bluebeard, as they sat at supper, told Fatima that early the next week he would be going on a journey to see a rich cousin of his. "And his name, my dear, is—what do you think?" He laughed aloud as he said it: "Why, Redbeard! Now, while I am away everything will be in your charge. Yours only, my poppet. And here are the keys."

Saying this, he drew out of his pouch a great jangling bunch of keys, large and small, and laid them on the table beside her plate. Then, one by one, he told Fatima which key was for which room, until he came to the last. "And *this* little key, my dear—*this* little key is for the room at the end of the stone corridor that leads to the

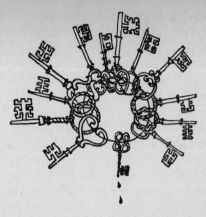

tower. Never stray in that direction. Don't go down there. It's cold; and there are draughts and rats. And on no account open the door at the end of the passage. That is a secret room. No eye looks into it, no foot crosses it but my own. My own," he repeated, stroking his blue beard, and looking at her down his long hooked nose out of his beady black eyes. "And I am sure if you do not do as I bid you about this room, you will agree that I should have good reason for being unutterably angry."

As he said that word *unutterably*, his eyes fairly sparkled in his head, and his beard seemed to bristle like the fur of a cat at sight of a dog. And seeing this, Fatima grew pale and trembled.

"There, there, pretty poppet!" he said, patting her hand as it lay on the table, "so long as you do what I tell you, no harm can come. I shall be home again in a few days."

By noon on the Tuesday he had set out in his coach, and Fatima waved a shawl from a window until he was out of sight. But days before he had gone, Fatima had sent a message to her sister Anne, entreating her to come and stay with her until Bluebeard returned. For she could not abide the thought of being alone in the house.

The next day, with Bluebeard's great bunch of keys in her hand, Fatima took Anne from room to room and showed her all the splendours of this house. In some of the great rooms there were chairs and tables of solid silver, with curtains of crimson velvet, and glass candelabra full of candles, and mirrors on the marble walls. In one much smaller room was a cage made of gold wires and cedarwood, and it was filled with singing birds of gold and silver with gems for eyes; and these birds sang when Fatima touched a secret spring. In other rooms was only emptiness—only the light from the windows, and dust and spiders' webs. One of the upper rooms, too, the very last they visited, contained nothing but an immense wardrobe of ebony, its shelves and hooks crammed with bonnets and gowns and furs and feathers and silk pelisses and petticoats and all kinds of finery.

"How strange," cried Anne at sight of these, "that such an old bachelor as Bluebeard was before you married him should have all these fine females' clothes!"

"I expect," said Fatima, "they belonged to his sisters."

"I wonder," said Anne.

So they went away from that room and down the wide staircase together. And Anne said, "So now we have seen everything?" But to this Fatima replied nothing, for, though she was pining and pining merely to peep into the little room at the end of the stone passage, she made no mention to her sister of the last little key of all, because she was afraid that Anne would think Bluebeard mistrusted her.

So time went on, until it came to the middle of the third night after Bluebeard had gone away. Then Fatima could bear herself no longer. She had not slept a wink for thinking of the secret room, and at last she rose up out of her bed, lit the candle in her silver candlestick, muffled herself up in a night-gown, and with the bunch of keys in her hand, crept downstairs and so came to the forbidden stone corridor. And as she hastened along with her light she could hear a wild scampering and scurrying; and the air was bitter cold and still in the passage. With one last glance over her shoulder, Fatima put the key into the lock and opened the door.

Its hinges were rusty, and as she opened it they made a dismal screeching noise, and Fatima's heart, at sound of it, stood still with terror. Yet when she looked into the room there was at first sight nothing to see—nothing but another heap of clothes, some old leather trunks, and an immense cupboard. For a while Fatima forgot her fears, and was bitterly disappointed.

Then, still greedy with curiosity, and with her candle in her hand, she stole over to the cupboard and opened the door. And, alas! what a sight met her eyes! She uttered a scream; the keys dropped from her hand; she almost swooned away. For there, hanging in a row, were what she knew at once must be Bluebeard's dead past wives, before she herself had become the last of them. And *now* Fatima realized where all those fine females' clothes had come from.

There Anne found her, for she had heard her cry, and the two sisters went back to Fatima's bedroom; but Fatima was so much terrified she could scarcely breathe or speak. At last Anne made her promise to say nothing to Bluebeard about the room when he returned; and she herself, even though it was not yet near daybreak, at once sent a messenger galloping off to their mother's house to bring back in all haste their two brothers who had but just returned from foreign parts. The rest of the night Anne spent with her sister Fatima, lying beside her in her bed, and trying in vain to make her warm again.

The first thing in the morning Fatima looked at the keys, and found, to her horror, that some of them had thick black stains upon them. She rubbed and scoured and polished away at them all that morning, but though she managed to get most of them perfectly clean, try as she might, she could not get one little black speck out of the key of the secret room, nor even could Anne either, though she had much stronger fingers and could rub far harder.

About noon two or three days afterwards, Fatima, watching out of the window, saw her husband's coach far away to the east, lumbering along like a great creeping insect over the country road. At this she ran hastily downstairs to her sister. "Alas, alas, Anne! He comes!" she said. When Bluebeard entered into the house, he kissed her on both cheeks, and she trembled.

Then he looked at her, and said, "Well, poppet, and where are the keys?"

So Fatima brought Bluebeard his great bunch of keys.

"Ah, ah!" says he, smiling, "what a busy wife we have! Eh? How prettily they shine!" Then again he looked at her with his little eyes and said:

"But what is this wee, wee little black speck, Fatima, on the key of the secret room?"

But Fatima could make no answer; she could only stare at him, quaking all over. At this silence, and seeing her with head hung down and trembling hands, Bluebeard's face blackened like a storm at sea. His blue beard seemed to bristle, and his eyes to sparkle.

"Ha!" he said. "I see you have disobeyed me, Fatima. I see you have discovered what happens to a wife who does what she is told *not* to do. Come with me; maybe we shall find room for you, too, in the secret chamber!" Then, in spite of her cries and lamentations, he at once dragged her out of the room and along the stone corridor. But there was one thing of which this wretch was not aware—that Fatima's sister Anne was in the house, and was now hidden in a little stone closet above the secret room, and was gazing out of its window in watch for her two brothers.

On the threshold of the room, Fatima fell upon her knees before Bluebeard, and, with tears raining from her eyes, entreated him. "Oh, my dear husband, mercy!" she said. "Give me but a little time in which to say a prayer before I die."

Bluebeard looked at her, and said, "Well, it must be short and quick. Seven minutes shall be yours; then hope no more. I will wait at the end of the corridor."

When he had gone back to the end of the stone corridor, leaving her alone, Fatima slipped into the room and almost for the first time in her life showed that she had some sense in her vain, silly head. For, once inside the room, she drew the bolt softly but swiftly, and so locked the door. And she called, "Sister Anne, Sister Anne, it is death in a moment. What do you see?"

And Sister Anne, looking out over the western road towards the setting sun, whispered, "Only an empty road, Fatima. No sign yet."

And Fatima in a little time cried again, "Sister Anne, Sister Anne, what do you see now?"

"I see a cloud of dust on the road," said Anne.

"Ah, they come, they come!" cried Fatima.

"No," answered Anne at last, "it is nothing but a flock of silly sheep, and the sun on their fleeces and the dust rising over them."

And Fatima in a little while cried again, "Sister Anne, Sister Anne, what do you see *now*?"

"I see dust again and a glinting—but oh, alas, Fatima, it is only the huntsmen with the hounds, and their hunting-horns shining."

By this time Bluebeard had heard Fatima's voice as she talked with her sister Anne, and his hand was upon the door. When he found it was locked and barred against him, his rage passed all bounds. He beat upon the door, until the bolt within began to strain and bend and buckle in its socket.

"Oh, Sister Anne, Sister Anne, what do you see *now*?" cried Fatima.

"I see horsemen," whispered Anne.

"Horsemen?"

"Ay, Fatima, horsemen—galloping! It is our brothers. They come, they come!"

With that she ran down the little flight of stone steps and clasped Fatima in her arms.

At this moment, after a last great wrench, the hasp of the door flew off, and there stood Bluebeard in his fury, in a sky-blue mantle, a great scimitar in his hand.

But hardly had he taken a step into the room when Fatima's two brothers came leaping down the corridor in pursuit of him, and in a moment or two his dead body lay stretched out upon the floor. So they buried his poor wives; and Fatima with her money went to live with her sister Anne. But the house upon the hill stood empty and vacant until at length it fell into ruin, desolation and decay.

Snow-White

O ne wintry afternoon—and snow was falling—a Queen sat at her window. Its frame was of the dark wood called ebony. And as she sewed with her needle she pricked her finger, and a drop of blood welled up on the fair skin. She raised her eyes, looked out of the window, and sighed within herself: "Oh that I had a daughter, as white as snow, her cheeks red as blood, and her hair black as ebony!"

By-and-by her wish came true, and she called the child Snow-White.

Some years afterwards this Queen died, and the King took another wife. She, too, was of a rare dark beauty, but vain and cold and proud. Night and morning she would look into her magic looking-glass and would cry softly:

> *"Looking-glass, looking-glass on the wall,*
> *Who is the fairest of women all?"*

And a voice would answer her out of the looking-glass:

"Thou, O Queen."

But as the years went by, Snow-White grew ever more lovely, and the Queen more jealous. And one day, when her waiting-women had dressed her hair and had left her, the Queen looked yet again into her looking-glass and whispered:

> "Looking-glass, looking-glass on the wall,
>   Who is the fairest of women all?"

And the voice from within it replied:

> "Fair, in sooth, art thou, O Queen;
>   But fairer than Snow-White is nowhere seen."

At this, the Queen was beside herself with rage and hatred; and in secret she sent for a huntsman, and bade him take Snow-White into the forest and do away with her.

The huntsman rode off with Snow-White into the marshy depths of the forest where the shade was so dense there was not a sound to be heard. But when he looked at her under the darkness of the trees, he had not the heart to do the Queen's bidding, and he reasoned within himself:

"Even if I leave her here in this forest, she may soon, alas! die of hunger. But kill her I cannot."

So, instead, he speared a wild boar, and dabbling Snow-White's kerchief in its blood, returned to the Queen. Snow-White, left alone in the forest, hastened on in terror. Soon night began to darken, and hearing the cries of roving beasts in the forest, she climbed up into the boughs of a tree, and there at last fell asleep. In the morning, when she awoke amidst the trees, there was a continual twittering of birds. Sunshine had dappled the green leaves and a butterfly had spread its wings upon her shoulder. Her courage came back to her. Having eaten some berries which she found clustering in the brambles and quenched her thirst in a brook, she set out once more to find her way out of the forest.

After wandering for many hours through its glades and dingles, she came at last to where, in a green hollow of the forest, as if at the edge of a saucer, was a long, low house with seven little lattice windows and seven small gables, and she tapped at the door. There came no answer. She tapped again, then lifted the latch and went in. And within was a room with wooden walls, and there was a fire smouldering on the hearth. In the middle of the room stood a table with seven little stools around it; while on the table itself lay seven platters and seven bowls, with seven spoons beside them, and seven tiny loaves of bread, and seven little glasses for wine. For it was so the Seven Dwarfs, whose house this was, always left it against their coming home in the evening.

Snow-White was footsore and hungry, and as she stood looking into this quiet room and nothing stirred in it but the smoke in the fireplace flowing up into the chimney, a few birds fluttered in through the open door, and hopping from platter to platter and twittering one to another, began picking up the crumbs and pecking at the loaves. Then thought Snow-White to herself: "What they must do often, perhaps I may do once."

So she broke off a mouthful from each tiny loaf in turn, and sipped a sip of wine from one of the glasses. Then she went upstairs, and came into another room of a like size to the room below, and with seven lattice windows under its gables. In this room were seven little beds, their sheets laundered white as snow. She sat down on one of the beds to rest herself; but from sitting slipped into lying, and then fell fast asleep.

Towards evening, the Seven Dwarfs came home with their sacks and picks and shovels from their copper-mines in the hills, and found their door ajar. They went in, and the first dwarf stood looking at his stool, which had been

pushed aside under the table; and he said: "Who has
been sitting on *my* stool?"

And the second looked and said: "Who has been
meddling with *my* platter?"

And the third looked and said: "Who has put crooked
my spoon?"

And the fourth looked and said: "Who has been
nibbling *my* bread?"

And the fifth looked and said: "Who has knocked
over *my* bowl?"

And the sixth looked and said: "Who has been drinking from *my* glass?"

And the seventh looked and said nothing, but climbed
up the stairs, and in a shrill voice called down to the other
dwarfs: "Aha! and what have I found lying on *my* bed?"

The dwarfs clustered together round the bed and
looked at Snow-White. In all their wanderings they had
never seen a lovelier face; and they let her sleep on. Now,
though Snow-White, when she woke up, was at first
afraid of the dwarfs with their queer looks and humpty
backs, they spoke kindly to her, asking her whence she
had come, and entreated her to stay with them.

Then Snow-White told them her story, and of how
her step-mother, the jealous Queen, had sent her into the
forest, and how the huntsman had abandoned her. The
dwarfs warned her against the Queen. The wicked, they
said, are never at rest. "Hide with us here, and you are
safe."

So Snow-White became the housekeeper of the dwarfs.
She made their beds, swept their room, prepared their
pot of broth in the evening, and poured out for them
their wild-fruit wine. They taught her how to knead
dough for bread, and what green things are good for
salad, and what roots and toadstools are fit for food. She

was happy with the Seven Dwarfs, and sang over her work with such delight that the birds of the forest would flock there in a multitude and sing too, and she fed them with her crumbs and scraps.

Now one day it seemed to the Queen, as she looked into her magic glass, that a faint line of care or foreboding had begun to show itself in the smoothness of her forehead, and she whispered:

> *"Looking-glass, looking-glass on the wall,*
> *Who is the fairest of women all?"*

And the voice from within replied:

> *"Fair in sooth, art thou, O Queen;*
> *But fairer than Snow-White is nowhere seen.*
> *Happy she lives, beyond words to tell,*
> *Where the dwarfs of the mountains of copper dwell."*

At this, the face looking back out of the glass at the Queen became so black and crooked with rage that she hardly knew herself. Next morning she questioned her women, and was told where the copper-mines were and in what mountains. Then she disguised herself and dressed herself up as a pedlar, and painted her cheeks, and put on a black wig and a cloak. In this disguise she came towards sunset to the house of the Seven Dwarfs, looking at it from out of the edge of the forest in its green hollow.

It chanced that Snow-White herself, having finished her day's work, was sitting at an upper window with a piece of sewing. There the Queen saw her, so drew near, and at last from below called softly:

"Any knick-knacks? Any laces or ribbons? Buckles for your shoes?"

Now Snow-White had been so happy with the dwarfs that she had forgotten the promise she had made them never to open the door to any stranger; and she went down and opened the door. The Queen spoke her fair, and flattered her. She showed her pretty stay-laces, twisted of green and scarlet silk, and said craftily: "Let *me* lace you up, my dear, and you shall look as trim as a blackbird."

But she laced her so swiftly and she laced her so tight, that poor Snow-White could scarcely breathe, and fell down on the threshold like one dead. There the dwarfs found her when they came home in the evening.

The first cried: "Our Snow-White is dead!" So, too, the second, and the third, and the fourth, and the fifth, and the sixth—all wailing, except the seventh, who, seeing how tightly her stays were laced, took his knife out of his belt and slit up the laces.

Sure enough, in a few moments the colour came stealing back into Snow-White's pale cheeks, and she sat up and smiled at them. When she was able to talk again, she told them all that had happened, and the dwarfs begged and entreated her never again to open the door to any stranger.

Late that night, the Queen in the moonlight learnt of her magic looking-glass that Snow-White was still alive, and she began to be afraid. Seven days after she again disguised herself. This time she wore a bright green cloak and a red wig, and with her painted cheeks and lips looked almost young and comely. When she came to the house of the dwarfs, she tapped at the door.

Snow-White, who was at that moment making bread, paused in her kneading, listened and called: "Who's there?"

Then the Queen looked in at her through the open window; and she was so changed in face and dress that Snow-White did not know or recognize her. So Snow-

White came to the window and feasted her eyes on the pretty trinkets and gewgaws which the Queen had set out on a tray from the pack she carried. At last the Queen drew out from under her skirts, and showed Snow-White, a comb for the hair, clear as amber, and of gold and tortoiseshell.

But Snow-White said: "I cannot buy it; I haven't money enough. Besides, I have promised."

And the Queen said: "Why! but come closer, my dear, and I myself will fix the comb in your hair, and you can look at yourself in that copper pan over there. La! in all my days I never saw hair so fine and sleek and lovely. Take the comb for love, my pretty; and pay for it when you please."

So Snow-White came close to the window, and the Queen thrust the comb into her hair, and the poison with which the Queen had prepared the comb was so potent that Snow-White swooned away at the window. Then the Queen—her face dark with malice and hatred—looked in upon her and thought to herself that now at last she was safe and that her mind could be at rest.

But once again when the dwarfs came home that evening, the seventh, who was the youngest of them and nimblest of wit, after eyeing her closely, at once drew out the tortoiseshell comb from her hair. And though Snow-White lay in a swoon for some hours longer, by midnight her senses had come back to her. She smiled out into the world again, and the dwarfs were so happy to have their beloved housekeeper safe once more, they hadn't the heart to chide her.

It was midnight when the Queen again looked into her glass. She whispered in triumph:

> "Looking-glass, looking-glass on the wall,
> Who is the fairest of women all?"

Then the voice from within it replied:

"Thy journey was in vain, O Queen,
Lovelier than Snow-White is nowhere seen."

At these words the Queen gnashed her teeth at the glass, and there and then she stole down from her bed-chamber to a little secret closet where she kept dangerous herbs and dyes and unguents, and with all her craft and skill she made a poisonous apple, rosy red on the one side, green on the other. The very sight of it made her mouth water, and she smiled to herself as she looked at it and thought: "This is the end."

For the third time she dressed up and disguised herself, but now as a very old woman, hunched and ragged, with a grey wig under her peaked hat. When a little before sunset she came to the house of the dwarfs, Snow-White was drawing water from the well, and as she stooped to pick up the bucket she heard the quavering voice of the pedlar. She ran in at once and drew the wooden bolt across the door; then went upstairs and peeped out of a window ajar. The Queen spied her up there, peering down from the window, and cackled softly:

"Ripe apples, ripe apples! Who'll buy my ripe apples?"

Snow-White, peeping, saw the apple in the old woman's hand; and riper, fairer apple she had never seen. But she shook her head, and the Queen said:

"Many more where these came from, dainty lady. Perhaps the seven little gentlemen would like an apple to their supper. See, I will cut this one in half, and you shall eat the rosy half, and I will have the green."

So saying, she cut the apple in half, and threw the rosy half up to the window. And Snow-White, thinking what pleasure such fruits as these would give the dwarfs, couldn't resist it, but caught the piece of apple, and lifted it to her nose to smell its sweetness. Then she took a bite, but before she could swallow it she fell down on the floor, and lay there, to all seeming, cold, leaden, and dead.

Yet again that midnight the Queen stole catlike to her looking-glass and whispered:

> *"Looking-glass, looking-glass on the wall,*
> *Who is the fairest of woman all?"*

The voice within cried hollowly: "Thou, O Queen!" But no more.

When the Seven Dwarfs came home that evening, their hearts were sad and dismal indeed. Nothing they could do brought any tinge of colour back into Snow-White's cheeks, or warmth to her fingers. She remained cold and mute and lifeless.

Yet they could not bear to think of hiding her away in the dark, cold ground, so, working all of them together, they made a coffin of glass, and put up a wooden bench not far from the house, and rested the glass coffin on it, mantling it with garlands of green leaves and flowers. The birds that Snow-White used to feed with her crumbs and scraps, seeing her lying there, safe and close in their company, now sang louder than ever. But there never came any sign that Snow-White heard. And the dwarfs marvelled at her beauty, for she lay still and cold as snow, and her hair black as ebony, though her cheeks were colourless as wax.

One fresh morning, when early summer was in the forest again, a Prince came riding with his huntsmen, and seeing this strange glass coffin on the bench, dismounted from his horse, and, pushing the green garlands aside, looked in at Snow-White lying there. His heart misgave him at sight of her, for he had never seen a face so lovely or so wan. He called to her, but she made no answer.

Then he bade his huntsmen sound their horns, but she never stirred. He waited there, with his huntsmen, until evening.

When, as of old, the dwarfs came home, he questioned them and asked them how long Snow-White had so lain in the glass coffin. They told him, and he said:

"My father, the King, has a leech who is wondrously skilled in magic herbs. Give me leave to carry off this coffin, and I promise you that, whether he is able to work a marvel or not, your Snow-White, if you wish it, shall come back to you alive and well, or sleeping on as she sleeps now."

The dwarfs talked together in grief and dismay at the thought of losing Snow-White, even though only for a few days. But having given the Prince of their bread and wine, they agreed at last that this should be so.

It was dark night when the huntsmen were drawing near the palace of the King, and one of them stumbled over the jutting root of a tree. By this sudden jarring of her glass coffin, the morsel of poisonous apple that was stuck in Snow-White's throat became dislodged. She lifted her head from her green pillow, coughed out the morsel, and cried: "God help me!"

The Prince, hearing her cry, looked in on her in the starlight, and took off the lid of the coffin. Then Snow-White sat up, and gazed at him as if ages and ages ago she had known him of old, but could not remember his name, for as yet he seemed but part of her long dreaming. She put out her hand and touched him.

The Prince rejoiced with all his heart, and sent back two of his huntsmen, who with their horns roused the dwarfs before daybreak, and gave them the glad news that Snow-White had come alive again; and that their master, the Prince, had bidden them all to the King's palace, for Snow-White, before falling into a deep sleep again, had talked only of them.

The King and Queen, having heard Snow-White's story, rejoiced with their son the Prince, and gave a banquet to welcome her; and the Seven Dwarfs sat at a table on stools of ebony, their napkins white as snow, and their wine red as blood. And Snow-White herself poured out wine for them just as she used to do.

As for the murderous Queen, hated and feared by all around her, she had become lean and haggard and dreaded even the thought of her magic looking-glass. In time she fell mortally sick, and was haunted continually, waking and dreaming, by remembrance of Snow-White who, she supposed, was long ago dead and forgotten. At last, in the dead of night she summoned one of her waiting-women and bade her take down the looking-glass from

the wall, and bring it to her bedside. Then she drew close the curtains round her bed, and whispered:

> "Looking-glass, looking-glass on the wall,
>   Who is the fairest of women all?"

And the voice within replied:

"*Fair, in sooth, wert thou, I ween,*
But Snow-White too is now a Queen.
Fairer than she is none, I vow.
Look at thyself! Make answer! Thou!"

At this, the looking-glass slipped out of her hand, and was dashed to pieces on the floor. Her blood seemed to curdle to ice in her body, and she fell back upon her pillows. There her ladies found her in the morning. But few Queens as evil as she was have died in their beds.

The Twelve Windows

—————————◄○●○►—————————

Once upon a time there was a Princess who was so dear to her father that he had but one care in his mind—the fear and foreboding that some day she would get married and leave him. Seeing how this continually haunted and troubled the King's mind—for the Princess loved him no less truly—she made him a vow. She vowed that she would never marry, not even a Prince of the Indies or a magician of Cathay, except only on one condition: that any suitor for her hand, whosoever he might be, must first so hide himself in her father's palace that within one single hour she would not be able to discover where.

Now this might not seem to be a very hard matter. In the King's palace there were rooms without number, not to speak of galleries, corridors, lofts, watching-nooks; bakehouse, buttery, chandlery, spicery; his kitchens, pantries, cellars, vaults, coffers, wardrobes, chests, ovens and wells. His park and gardens and orchards were green and shady with a multitude of mighty forest trees and flowering bushes in which the birds of the air, of every feather and song, might all be perched yet none be seen.

This being so, how could any mortal creature, with but two eyes to see with, hope within one single hour to discover a hider's hiding-place? But this Princess was not like other princesses, for she had eyes with the witching power of being able to spy out and detect everything within the circuit of the royal palace—a creeping snail under a wall, an ant with its egg, or a queen bee among her maidens. In order that she might practise these witching eyes of hers, a marvellous chamber had been made, its walls of cherry-wood and ebony. This chamber was built high aloft above the topmost roof of the palace, and in it were twelve windows of carved stone and crystal. From these the Princess could look out on all sides of her to the very outskirts of the world, to the far, high mountains in the east, and to the low, flat, blue sea to the west.

Not only had she vowed she would never marry any suitor unless he could hide himself where she could not find him; but that if he failed to do so, he should lose his head.

Nevertheless, this Princess was so renowned for her beauty that noble young men from far countries, and wise ones of the East, daring the fate decreed, had journeyed to her father's kingdom hoping to win her in marriage. But none yet had hidden where she had been unable to find him, and none had returned to the place from which he had set out.

Now, there was a young swineherd that kept pigs in the forest a league or two from the King's palace; and the high-road through the forest ran not far away from the hut in which he lay at night. Ever and again he would watch these Princes from afar come proudly riding in their fine raiment and with their retinue of servants around them in all the colours of the rainbow, on their way to the palace. But not one of these had he ever seen return.

His forefathers had been keepers of pigs in the great forest for hundreds of years before him. And living alone with his pigs (which are by nature knowing, crafty and clever creatures), and sitting for hours together with only his own thoughts for company, this young swineherd had grown wise for his age, and was as brave and bold as he was wise.

He had asked questions, too, of every traveller that came his way, and had been told that it was no matter whether a man was of noble or common blood, good looks or bad, blind or lame or rich or poor. Let him but hide himself so cunningly that the Princess from her chamber with the twelve windows should be unable to discover him, his reward should be the lovely one herself.

What wonder, then, as he sat alone by his fire in the forest when the nights were cold, he would dream of her beauty, and pine to try his luck! Better no head at all, he would think to himself, than a heart in terror of losing it.

So having at last made up his mind, he left his pigs and set off at once to the palace. But when he came to the watchman at the gates of the palace and told him what he had come for, the watchman burst out laughing. Princes and soothsayers and noblemen he knew of old, but this young swineherd in his ragged clothes, his face roasted by the sun, with his thick thatch of hair—he had never seen his like before.

None the less, the watchman had been given orders that it mattered not who might come on this bold quest, he should be brought instantly into the Princess's presence. In spite, too, of the swineherd's rags and his broken shoes and unkempt hair, there was a look in his face, and something in the way he spoke, that took the liking of the watchman. When too he found that all his attempts to dissuade him from his folly only made him the more eager and resolved, he said no more.

"Pity it is, young man," he told him, "to lose your

head before it has become used to being on your shoulders. But keep up your courage, and I'll help you all I can."

So he dressed the swineherd in an old cloak of scarlet and green, that had belonged to his son who was killed in the wars. He gave him a hood of squirrel's fur to cover his head, and shoes of fine leather to put on his feet. Then he took the swineherd to the Princess.

The Princess looked at the swineherd with her clear, shining eyes and spied out instantly the rags beneath his cloak of green and scarlet, and the thick, tousled hair tucked under his hood. But he, having gazed but a moment into her eyes, turned his own away. Yet she had seen the wild blue light in them, and heard his heart knocking on his ribs; and of all the strangers who had come to the palace in hope to win her love, this swineherd was the first the Princess had ever pitied for his own sake alone.

"Indeed," she thought to herself, "this young man who seems by his looks to have come straight out of the greenwood, and always to have been alone with the sun and the wild deer and the stars, must have a rare courage to attempt to win what even mighty princes and wizards of the East have paid for so dearly."

Then she looked at him again out of her clear, shining eyes, and spoke gently to him: "Would it not be a sad and miserable mischance," she asked him, "to die after having lived for so few years, for the vow I have made is one that cannot be broken?" He heard, but shook his head.

Indeed at sound of her voice the young man could scarcely believe his ears, it was so sweet and clear. It was like water at summertime in a well. And seeing how gently she had spoken to him, he made bold to ask her a favour, which was this: That he should be allowed to make not one, but three attempts to hide himself, and each of these on three different days.

"One learns by practice, lady, even in the tending of swine," he said, "and I—well——" But he could say no more. At this the Princess was grieved at heart, yet happy, and she willingly granted him this favour. Then with a scarf of gold tissue the Princess hid her eyes, while the swineherd went off to hide.

He hastened down and asked his friend the watchman in which of the dungeons of the palace he would be shut up if he failed—before, that is, his head was cut off. "Where did the other wretches lie groaning," he asked him, "who had lost the one thing in the world I pine for and must have?"

The watchman looked at him, and seeing his young, simple face, pitied him; and himself led him down a staircase hewn out of the solid rock into the deepest of the King's dungeons, where even the sun at noonday brought only a pallid gloom into its murk, and there he covered him up with straw.

In due time, and as she had promised, the Princess opened her eyes again. She looked out of the first window of her chamber: nobody there. She looked out of the second: nobody there either; and then from the third, and still found nothing. And so to the fourth and to the fifth. At each window her heart grew ever more glad. But at the seventh window she cast her glance downward, and with her eyes of witchery perceived the young man huddled up under the straw in the furthermost corner of the dungeon. And she sighed.

Nevertheless, though he had failed this first time, the swineherd was of good courage. On his journey back to his pigs in the forest he never stopped thinking, except when the lovely face of the Princess came between him and his thoughts. All that evening he spent swimming and diving in a clear green pool that lay under the beech-trees in the forest near his hovel; a pool in which, when its waters were still, every young silken green leaf on the boughs above its waters showed clear as in a looking-glass.

The next day he awoke before daybreak and returned at once to the pool. And at evening he came again to the palace. The Princess received him with an even gentler courtesy, and entreated him to dare no further. But this only put all other thoughts out of his mind, and this time he went out and, having first filled his lungs with by far the longest breath of his lifetime, he plunged into the deepest of the King's fish-ponds. There he lay, deep down under the water-lilies, clinging to their writhen roots in the ooze of the pool. These were the longest minutes the swineherd had ever known, longer even than when he had lain huddled under the straw in the dungeon.

In due time the Princess looked out of her first window, and saw nought of him; and out of the second and still nought; and when she had come to the tenth and still had utterly failed to discover where the swineheard lay hidden, she rejoiced. But at the eleventh window, looking towards the south, her heart misgave her. For plain as in a dream she could see the young man cowering beneath the lilies in the ooze of their roots, and his cloak hidden under a bush of broom nearby. With all his craft he had failed; and she had triumphed. Yet she sighed, and then sighed again.

That evening the swineheard, trusting to his own wits no longer, went off into the forest to the abode of a certain Fox—a Fox that one winter's morning a year or two before this he had saved from the snow. Sitting there in the dusky forest, he told the Fox his trouble, for this creature was known to all forest-folk as the wisest fox in the whole world, and one that knew wizardry.

The Fox listened in patience to his story, then stayed motionless, his nose pointing due north and his brush spread out behind him due south, while he debated within himself. At length his eyes blinked, his ears twitched. A plan had come into his wise head.

"Sleep here until morning," he bade the swineherd, "and lie close to the westward of that bush, for soon the wind will be changing; and I'll have speech with thee at dawn."

At daybreak the Fox appeared again, and merrily greeted the swineherd, bidding him be of good cheer. "Stoop down, my friend," said he; and when the swineherd had stooped low beside him, the Fox brushed him all over, head to heel, with his brush. There was a sweet strange breath in the air as of wild herbs, and there and then, the swinehead was changed by the Fox's magic into a white mountain hare, of a fur soft as wool, and eyes blue as ice in the morning.

The Fox then brushed himself nose-tip to stern with his brush, and became the very similitude of an old man in a sheep-skin. Then he took up the hare into his arms, and went into the town. It was market-day and there was a fair. At some distance from the beating of the drums and the piping and the press of people, the Fox took up his station close to the entry of the market-place which was nearest to the King's palace. Here he waited patiently in the posture of a blind man begging for alms, the mountain hare clasped close within his arms.

Now the Princess at this hour, as the Fox well knew, was sitting in her ebony and cherry-wood chamber, with its twelve windows of carved stone and crystal, and she was looking out towards the town. But the beauty of her face was now sad and downcast, and her thoughts were not with what she looked on; for her eyes were fixed like the eyes of a sleep-walker.

But at last, as she gazed on at the moving throng of busy and merry country folk with their children at the fair, hastening to and fro like ants in an ant-heap in the heat of summer, she became aware of this old man, standing motionless in his sheep-skin, as heedless of the cries and bustle around him as if he were made of wood, and with the snow-white mountain hare couched in his arms.

He stood there stock-still as though he were alone in a wilderness; and the hare might have been of ivory, with eyes of emerald, in his arms. The Princess had never seen the like before. So she sent one of her waiting-women to enquire of the old man what he did there, and whence he had come. When the waiting-woman returned to the palace, she told the Princess that the old man was either dumb or could make no sense of her questionings, being, as it seemed, a stranger to her language; but that never had she seen a little creature more beautiful than the hare he had in his arms. "It has eyes blue as sapphires, and fur softer than silk."

At this, the Princess was filled with desire to possess the hare, and again sent out her waiting-woman, who bought the hare from the old man (for so he looked), for seven pieces of silver.

Now the day before, the swineherd had told the Princess that he would not himself appear before her again in her chamber, but would hide himself on the very stroke of three the next afternoon.

"For I think," he said, "even if I trod softer than a shadow, the sound of my footsteps might be heard as I go down the staircase. Not even my heart stops beating a

moment, lady, but you seem to know of it! To-morrow, then, by your grace, I will not enter into the palace at all."

The Princess had smiled at him and said: "Let that be so." She entreated him, too, to hide himself with all the cunning, care and skill he could. "For this time is the last time," she said; nor could she do otherwise, for such was the King's decree. But the Fox, when he and the swineherd had sat talking and communing together in the early morning, had told the young man what do to.

Now a little before the hour agreed on between the swineherd and the Princess, she sat fondling the hare in her lap, nor would she now have parted with it for seventy times seven pieces of silver; and the hare (as the Fox had counselled it), presently crept up and concealed itself beneath the thick strands of her golden hair.

At three o'clock the Princess, having forgotten even that the little creature shared her secret chamber with her, bandaged her eyes with three silk scarves, one of gold, one of silver, and one bright blue; and she sealed up her ears lest even a whisper should reach them.

At last she rose and looked out of the first window. Nothing there. Then out of the second. Nothing there. Then out of the third. Nought there neither. And so on and on. At the eleventh window it seemed her heart would stop beating; and at last she came to the twelfth. One swift, keen, circling glance she cast about her out of her dark, clear eyes, but of the swineherd whom she so greatly feared to see she saw not a trace. Then she sat down with joy in her chair and wept. For the one thing even eyes of witchery cannot do is to see behind them.

The little hare, not daring to stay even for an instant to comfort her, ran out into the forest, and the Fox, having with all haste and expedition brushed him over with his brush, changed him back into his own shape again.

Then the young swineherd thanked the Fox beyond measure, and gathered some bright, ripe, wild fruit in the forest and put it into a wicker basket with green leaves over it. Next he chose out of his young pigs the sleekest and the fattest, and with this under his arm and his basket in hand, he went back to the palace and to the Princess. The Princess laughed to see him and took the little pig on to her lap; and it squeaked, and she laughed again. Then she began to weep a little—for sheer joy—and turned away.

At this the King looked at the young man as if he would that he had twenty heads, and that he himself might have the pleasure of lopping every one of them off. But when he heard that the swineherd lived in the forest, and had no wish to carry off the Princess into a far country, he was greatly comforted.

What is more, the swineherd answered the King's questions with such modesty and good sense, and his manners were so simple and open and free, that, taking him all in all, the King was heartily pleased with him.

So he led the young man by the hand, and presented him to the Princess. At which the little pig squeaked for the third time; but the swineherd said nothing, for he could think of nothing to say.

Clever Grethel

There was once a cook, and her name was Grethel. She wore shoes with red rosettes on them, and when she went walking in these shoes she would turn herself this way and that, saying: "Well I never, you *are* a handsome creature!"

At night as she combed her hair in the glass she would say: "My! so there you are!" And they called her "clever Grethel".

Whenever after a walk she came home to her master's house again, she would always take a little sippet of wine. "You see, Grethel, my dear, it makes the tongue able to *taste* better," she would say. "And what's a cook without a tongue?" In fact, Grethel kept her tongue very busy, nibbling and tasting.

Now one day her master said to her: "I have a guest coming this evening, Grethel, and a guest that knows what's what, and I want you to roast us a pair of fowls for supper. Two, mind you, young and tender. And I want 'em roasted to a turn."

Grethel said: "Why, yes, master. They shall taste so good you won't know what you're eating."

So she killed two fowls, scalded and plucked them, tucked in their legs with a little bit of liver in between, stuffed them with stuffing, and towards evening put them down to a clear, red fire to roast. She basted and basted

166

them, and when they were done to a turn and smelt sweet as Arabia, and their breasts were a rich, clear, delicate brown, Grethel called out to her master:

"If that guest of yours don't come soon, master, I shall have to take the fowls away from the fire. And I warn you, they will be utterly spoilt, for they are just at their juiciest."

Her master said: "So, so! I will run out and see if he is coming."

As soon as her master had turned his back, Grethel thought to herself she would have another sip of something to drink. Having had one sip, she took another sip, and then another. Then she basted the fowls again, and twisted the spit. She puffed with the heat, the fire blazing in her face. Suddenly, as she stood looking at the fowls, she thought to herself: "Now cooking's cooking! I shouldn't wonder if them birds taste as good as they smell. Oh, oh, oh! It's a sin. It's a shame!"

Then she looked out of the window; and when she saw that nobody was coming, she said to herself: "There! what did I tell you? And lawks! one of the wings is burning." So she cut off the wing with a twist of her sharp knife, and holding it between her finger and thumb, ate every scrap of it up, to the very bone.

Then, "Dear me," she sighed to herself, looking at the chicken, "that one wing left looks like another wing missing!" So she ate up the other. Then she took another sip of wine, and once more looked at the fowls.

"Now think what a sad thing," she said. "Once those two poor hens were sisters, and you couldn't tell 'em apart. But now look at them: one whole and the other nowt but legs!" So she gobbled up the wings of the other chicken to make the pair look more alike. And still her master did not come. Then said she to herself:

"Lor', Grethel, my dear, why worry? There won't be any guest to-night. He has forgotten all about it. And master can have some nice dry bread and cheese." With that she ate up completely one of the chickens, skin, stuffing, gravy and all, and then, seeing how sad and lonely the other looked all by itself with its legs sticking up in the air and both its wings gone, she finished off that too.

She was picking the very last sweet morsel off its wishbone when her master came running into the kitchen, and cried: "Quick, Grethel! Dish up! dish up! Our guest has just turned the corner."

At this moment she was standing in front of the fire in her fine shoes and great cooking apron, and she looked over her shoulder at her master. But he at once rushed out to see if the table was ready, and the wine on it; snatched up the great carving-knife, and began to sharpen it on the doorstep.

Pretty soon after, the guest came to the door and knocked. Grethel ran softly out, caught him by the sleeve, pushed him out of the porch, pressed her finger on her lips, and whispered: "Ssh! Ssh! on your life! Listen, now, and be off, I beseech you! My poor master has gone clean out of his senses at your being so late. Mad! mad! If he catches you, he will cut your ears off. Hark now! He is sharpening his knife on the doorstep!"

At this the guest turned pale as ashes, and hearing the steady rasping of the knife on the stone, ran off down the street as fast as his legs could carry him. As soon as he was out of sight, Grethel hastened back to her master.

"La, master!" she said, "*you've* asked a nice fine guest to supper!"

"Why," says he, looking up with the knife in his hand, "what's wrong with him?"

"Wrong!" says she. "Why, he had scarce put his nose in at the door, when he gives a sniff. 'What! chicken!' says he, 'roast chicken!' And away he rushed into the kitchen, snatched up my two poor beeootiful birds, and without even waiting for the dish or the gravy, ran off with them down the street."

"What, *now?*" said her master.

"This very minute!" said Grethel.

"Both?" said her master.

"Both," said she.

"Heaven save us!" said her master. "Then I shall have nothing for supper!" And off he ran in chase of his guest, as fast as he could pelt, crying out as he did so:

"Hi, there! Stop! Stop! Hi! Just one! Just one! Only one!"

But the guest, hearing these words, and supposing that the madman behind him with his long knife meant one of his ears, ran on faster than ever into the darkness of the night.

And Grethel sat down, happy and satisfied. She gave one deep sigh, looked solemnly at the two bright red rosettes on her shoes, and had another sip or two of wine.

Rumplestiltskin

Once upon a time there was a poor miller who had a beautiful daughter. He loved her dearly, and was so proud of her he could never keep from boasting of her beauty. One morning—and it was all showers and sunshine and high, bright, coasting clouds—a stranger came to the mill with a sack of corn to be ground, and he saw the miller's daughter standing by the clattering mill-wheel in the sunshine. He looked at her, and said he wished he had a daughter as beautiful as she. The miller rubbed his mealy hands together, and looked at her too; and, seeing the sunbeams glinting in her hair, answered almost without thinking:

"Ay! She's a lass in a thousand. She can spin straw into gold."

Now this saying was quickly spread abroad, and at last reached the ears of the King, who, in astonishment at such a wonder, at once sent for the miller, and bade him bring his daughter with him.

"It has been told me," said the King, "this maid here can spin straw into gold. So she shall. But if she fails, then look to it! You shall hang from your own mill."

The miller was so shaken with fear of the King that his tongue stuck in his throat, and he could make no answer.

Then the King went in secret and led the miller's daughter into a byre, where his cows were housed, and in which lay two or three bundles of straw. He looked at the miller's daughter and smiled. "There," said he, "you have straw enough. Spin that into gold before morning." Having said this, with his own hand he locked the door, and left her to herself.

She looked at the spinning-wheel, and she looked at the straw; and at thought of what would happen on the morrow, she cried, "O Father! Father!" and burst into tears. And as she sat there weeping, there was a rustling, and again a rustling, and out from under the straw there came and appeared a little midget of a man, with a peaked hat on his head, long lean shanks, a red nose, and a rusty-coloured beard that swept down even below his belt.

"What's all this crying about?" he asked angrily. "I can't get a minute's peace for it."

She was so surprised at sight of him that she stopped crying and told him all.

He jeered at her. "Spin straw, forsooth! That's no matter. But what will you give me if *I* spin for you?"

The miller's daughter gazed at the dwarf through her tears. She had never before seen so odd and ugly a little man. But he looked back at her out of his needle-sharp eyes with such cunning that she half believed he could do what he said. She promised to give him her coral necklace. With that, he flicked his fingers in the air, took off his hat, sat down on the three-legged milking-stool in front of the wheel, put his foot on the treadle and began to spin.

Whrr, whrr, whrrr! The straw seemed to fly through the air, as if caught up in a wind. And in a moment, behold! one reel was filled. Round and round buzzed the wheel again—*whrr, whrr, whrrr, whrrrr*—and another reel was filled. Then a third and then a fourth. Soon all the straw was gold; the reels were heaped neatly together; the byre was swept empty.

The little man got down from his stool as fresh as a daisy, poked the coral necklace into the little pouch he carried, and off he went.

When next morning the King saw the reels of thread, and all of pure gold, he was mightily pleased, and he marvelled. But his greed for more grew with every glance at them. "Well and fair," said he, "well and fair. But little's but little. You shall try again."

Then once more in secret he shut up the miller's daughter in a stable, at least half of which was filled with straw. "Spin that into gold," he said, "and you shall have praise indeed. Fail me—then . . . but why think of that!"

For as the King looked at the miller's daughter he saw how simple and beautiful she was, and in his heart of hearts he pitied her a little, though he said nothing. He turned on his heel, went out of the stable, barred the door, and left her to herself.

The miller's daughter was in despair. Yesterday's straw was but as a handful compared with a basketful. She looked at the wheel, she looked at the straw, and cried to herself: "Oh, but, if only that little, long-nosed man were here again!"

None the less, she sat down at the wheel and tried to spin. But spin she couldn't, for the straw in her fingers only straw remained. "No hope! no hope! no hope!" she thought; but while these words were still in her mind, he dwarf came and appeared again out of the straw.

"Ah-ha!" says he. "What's amiss now?" She told him.

"And what will you give me *this* time, if I spin for you?" he said. She promised him the silver ring on her finger.

Down he sat, flung his beard over his shoulder, and with a flick of his fingers began to spin. *Whrr, whrr, whrrr,* went the wheel. The straw seemed to slide like melted metal through the air. The reels multiplied. The great heap steadily grew smaller; and long before dawn the straw was all gold, the reels were piled together, and the King's stable, with its mangers and stone water-trough, was as neat as a pin.

The King could hardly believe his eyes; but even yet his greedy mind was not satisfied. Still, he openly smiled at the miller's daughter, and said: "Well and fair! Well and fair, indeed! Only one more night's work, my dear, and your trial is over."

Then he took her again in secret into a barn which was heaped up almost to its thatched roof-beams with bundles of wheat-straw.

"Spin *that* into gold for me," he said, "and to-morrow you shall be Queen." With a glance over his shoulder, he went out, barred and bolted the door, and left her to herself.

The miller's daughter sat down. She looked at the spinning-wheel. She looked at the vast heap of straw.

"Ah," she said to herself, "to spin *that* into gold would take a hundred little long-nosed men."

"What, what, what!" cried a voice at the latch-hole, and in an instant little Master Long-Nose appeared once more, his eyes like green beads and his cheeks like crab-apples. But this night the miller's daughter had nothing left to offer him for wages. The dwarf looked at her, like a thrush looking at a snail. Then he said:

"*In the seed is the leaf and the bud and the rose,*
But what's in the future, why, nobody knows.

"See here, pretty maid: promise me your first child if

you ever have one, and Queen you shall be to-morrow."

The miller's daughter could only smile at this, having no belief at all that such a thing could ever be; and she promised him. Whereupon the dwarf snapped his fingers in triumph in the air, span round nine times on his toe, and at once sat down to the wheel, foot on treadle. *Whrr, whrrr, whrrrr*, went the wheel like a droning of bees in midsummer. *Whrr—whrrr—whrrrr—whrrrrr—whrrrrrr—* and a few minutes before the sun rose next morning the barn was swept clean as a whistle and the straw all gold. Then off he went.

The King kept his word. He never even asked the miller's daughter the secret of her skill—for that, too, he had promised her. And though his Queen was of birth so lowly, few Queens have been as beautiful; and fewer still have brought their husbands such a vast quantity of gold.

Some time afterwards, the Queen sat playing with her baby one May morning in the orchard of the King's palace. And as she played, sometimes she laughed, sometimes she danced, and sometimes she sang, for she was happy. But all in a moment her happiness was changed to fear and dread, for—as if he had sprung clean out of the trunk or bole of a crooked old apple-tree nearly—there stood the dwarf.

The dwarf looked at the Queen, and looked at her baby. "Ah-ha! A pretty thing!" he said. "And mine!"

Now the Queen had been so long happy and at peace that she had almost forgotten the promise she had made in her trouble. She gazed at the dwarf and pleaded with him. She vowed she would give him anything else in the world he wished, if only he would release her from her promise.

"Nay, nay!" said he at last, "a Princess is a Princess,

and a promise is a promise. Still, dame, as you haven't tried to cheat me, I'll make another bargain, with you. You shall have three days, and nine guesses. If at the end of the third and at the ninth you cannot tell me my name, then the child shall be mine."

And off he went.

The Queen thought and thought. She thought all night long, without a single wink of sleep. Hundreds of names came into her mind. At morning she went out in despair alone into the orchard, and at the very height of noon the dwarf popped out again from behind the old apple-tree.

"Ah-ha!" said he. "And what's my name, ma'am?"

The Queen guessed. First she said, "Abracadabra."

The dwarf shook his head. Next she said, "Catalawam-pus." The dwarf shook his head. Her third guess was just as the word came into her head, "Nickerruckerubble-grubb!" For she was at her wits' end.

The dwarf broke into a wild hoot of laughter, clapped his hands, looked down his nose, squeaked, "Try again"! and off he went.

All that night the Queen lay wide awake, a glimmering light beside her bed. Thrice she crept out and stooped over the ivory cradle where her baby lay asleep. It lay so placid and still it might have been of wax. But each time she returned to her bed she lay staring up into the blue silk canopy that tented it in, and thought of all the names she had ever heard of when she lived with her father at the mill. And at noon next morning once more the dwarf appeared.

"Ah-ha!" says he. "Three and three makes six, ma'am!"

First the Queen guessed, "Sheepshanks." Next she guessed, "Littlebody." And last she guessed, "Long-Nose."

The dwarf danced in derision, clapped his hands, looked down his nose, yelped in triumph, "Try again!" and off he went.

The Queen hastened back at once to the palace and sent for a messenger or courier who was swift of foot, sharp of hearing, and as keen of eye as hawk or raven. She sat in secret and told him what the little dwarf looked like, with his lean shanks, his red nose, his long rusty beard, and the hump on his back; and she bade the courier ride like the wind all the next night long in search of him, and to bring back only his name.

"Tell me his name," she said, "and seven bags of money shall be yours. Fail me, then never return again!"

The courier lost not a moment. All night he rode hither and thither, and this way and that. He pressed on into the very back-most parts of the kingdom, and came galloping out on the other side. At last, a little before daybreak, when dark was deepest and the moon had long since set in the west, he found himself at the parting of the ways where there is a mountain. Now it is there the Fox and the Hare greet each other as they pass at dawn.

And not far beyond these cross-roads the courier came to a little house. It was round as a molehill, with a roof of reed-thatch, while out of it there came the sound of singing. The courier dismounted from his horse, crept near, and peeping cautiously through the window, spied into the room within. There he saw a little, hunched-up man, with lean shanks, a long nose, and a rusty red beard that spread down even to his belt. He was dancing and singing before a fire that burnt merrily in the hearth; and as he danced, these were the words he sang:

> "This morn, I baked, this night I brew—
> A wizard I, of mighty fame;
> But nobody never nowhere knew
> That Rumple—— is my name."

But listen as closely as he dared, the courier could not be certain of the sound of the last two syllables after that *Rumple*, though he knew well this must be the little dwarf the Queen had sent him out to find. Rumple, Rumple—he was certain of *that*. But what then? *Stinzly? Stimpsky? Stitchken?*—he tried in vain.

He brooded within himself a moment, and then began mimicking softly with his mouth the call of a little owl at the window. Sure enough, when the dwarf within heard the owl calling he began to sing and dance again. And as he danced these were the words he said:

> "*Some live lone as fox and bird,*
> *But who's to aid my Royal Dame,*
> *For nobody never nowhere heard*
> *That Rumplestiltskin is my name.*"

At this, the messenger (rejoicing beyond measure) got down from the window, took some bread and meat out of his saddlebag, and sat down by the wayside. There, leaving his horse to browse on the crisp mountain grasses under the last stars, he ate his supper (and breakfast), and while he did so repeated the name he had heard over and over to himself, until he was as sure of it as of his own. Then he mounted his horse and galloped back to the palace.

The next day, the Queen attired herself in a green mantle and put a garland of flowers in her hair; and she sat down in the orchard alone to await the coming of the dwarf. At the very stroke of noon he popped out as usual from behind the mossy old apple-tree, and this time he wore a peacock's feather stuck in his hat.

"Ah-ha!" says he. "Three more guesses, ma'am, and the Princess is mine." Because of his old kindness to her, the Queen pleaded with him, promising him any treasure he might desire except this one only. But he grew angry and even uglier:

> "*A bargain's a bargain; a vow's a vow*
> *To the very last doit of it. Answer me now.*"

The Queen smiled, and first she guessed, "Wheat-Straw."

He laughed.

Next she guessed, "Reels of Gold."

He laughed louder. Then for her last and ninth guess the Queen lifted her chin, laughed too, and whispered: "Now how about *Rumplestiltskin*, then?"

The dwarf stared at her as if in a wink he had been turned to stone. Then he trembled all over, head to foot, with rage, and stamped on the ground with such force that his lean shank pierced into it up to his very thigh. In fury, he caught at his other leg, trying in vain to wrench himself free. But his leg among the apple-roots, was clamped so fast, and he tugged so furiously, that he tore himself clean into two pieces. And that was the end of Rumplestiltskin.

The Sleeping Beauty

There lived long ago a King and a Queen, who, even though they loved one another, could not be wholly happy, for they had no children. But at last, one night in April—and a thin wisp of moon was shining in the light of the evening sky—a daughter was born to them. She was a tiny baby, so small that she could have been cradled in a leaf of one of the water-lilies in the moat of the castle. But there were no bounds to the joy of the King and Queen.

In due time they sent out horsemen all over the country, to invite the Fairy Women to her christening. Alas, that one of them should have been forgotten! There were wild hills and deep forests in that country, and it was some days before everything was ready. But then there was great rejoicing in the castle, and all day long came the clattering of horses' hoofs across the drawbridge over the moat, and not only horses, but much stranger beasts of burden, for some of the Fairy Women had journeyed from very far away. And each of them brought a gift—fine, rare, and precious—for the infant Princess.

When the merriment was nearly over, and most of the guests were gone, and the torches were burning low in the great hall, a bent-up old Fairy Woman—the oldest and most potent of them all—came riding in towards the castle on a white ass, with jangling bells upon its harness and bridle.

Without pausing or drawing rein, she rode on, over the drawbridge, and into the hall, nor stayed her ass until it stood beside the great chair where sat the chief nurse of the Princess, the infant asleep on a velvet cushion on her lap. The ass lifted its head and snuffed at the golden tassel of the cushion, as if it might be hay. Long and steadfastly this old Fairy Woman gazed down on the harmless child, lying asleep there, and her rage knew no bounds. At last she raised her eyes, and glaring round on the King and Queen from under the peak of her black mantle, she uttered these words:

> *"Plan as you may, the day will come,*
> *When in spinning with spindle, she'll prick her thumb.*
> *Then in dreamless sleep she shall slumber on*
> *Till years a hundred have come and gone."*

Then, mantling herself up again, she clutched at her bridle-rein, wheeled her jangling ass about in the hall, rode off, and was gone.

Now, if the King and Queen had remembered to invite this revengeful Fairy Woman to the Christening Feast, all might have been well. But to grieve at their folly was in vain. The one thing left to them was to keep unceasing watch over the child, and to do all in their power to prevent what the old Fairy Woman had foretold from coming true. The King sent messengers throughout his kingdom far and near, proclaiming that every spindle in his realm should be destroyed or brought at once to the castle. There they were burnt. Anyone after that who was found to be hiding a spindle away at once lost his head.

Many years went by, until the King and Queen seldom

recalled what the evil-wishing Fairy Woman had said. The Princess, as she grew up, first into a child, then into a maid, became ever more beautiful; and she was of a gentle nature, loving and lovable. Indeed, because they feared to sadden her heart with the thought that anyone had ever boded ill of her, she was never told of what had happened after her christening, or of the Fairy Woman on the white ass.

Now, nothing more delighted the young Princess than to wander over the great castle and to look out of its many windows, and to peep out through the slits in its thick walls. But there was one turret into which for a long time she never succeeded in finding her way. She would look up at it from the green turf beneath and long to see into it. Everywhere else she had been, but not there.

However, one evening in April she came by chance to a secret door that she had never till then noticed. There was a key in its iron lock. Glancing over her shoulder, she turned the key, opened the door, and ran as fast as she could up the winding stone steps beyond it.

Every now and then appeared a window-slit, and at one she saw the bright, young, new moon in the sky, like a sickle of silver; and at another the first stars beginning to prickle into the east. But at the top of the staircase she came to another door.

Here she stooped to peep through the latch-hole, and in the gloom beyond she saw an old, grey, stooping woman hunched up in a hood of lamb's-wool. She was squatting on a stool, and now she leant a little this way and now she leant a little that way, for with her skinny fingers she was spinning flax with a spindle.

The Princess watched her intently, and at last, though she was unaware of it, breathed a deep sigh at the latch-hole, for the sight of the twirling spindle had so charmed her mind that her body had almost forgotten to breathe.

At sound of this sigh the old woman at once stayed in her spinning, and, without moving, apart from tremulous head and hand, called softly:

> *"If thou wouldst see an old woman spin,*
> *Lift up the latch and enter in!"*

The Princess, knowing of no harm, lifted the latch and went in.

It was cold and dark in the thick-walled room, and when she drew near, the old woman began again to croon over her work; and these were the words she said:

> *"Finger and thumb you twirl and you twine,*
> *Twisting it smooth and sleek and fine."*

She span with such skill and ease, her right hand drawing the strands from the cleft stick or distaff, while her left twisted and stayed, twisted and stayed, that the Princess longed to try too.

Then the old woman, laying her bony fingers (that were cold as a bird's claws) on the Princess's hand, showed her how to hold the spindle, and at last bade her take it away and practise with it, and to come again on the morrow. But never once did she raise her old head from beneath her hood or look into the Princess's face.

For some reason which she could not tell, the Princess hid the spindle in a fold of her gown as she hastened back to her room. But she had been gone longer than she knew, and already the King and Queen were anxiously looking for her and were now come for the second time to her room seeking her. When they saw her, safely returned, first they sighed with relief, and then they began to scold her for having been away so long without reason.

And the Princess said: "But surely, mother, what is there to be frightened of? Am I not old enough yet to take care of myself?"

She laughed uneasily as (with the spindle hidden in the folds of her gown) she sat on her bedside, her fair hair dangling down on to its dark blue quilted coverlet.

The King said: "Old enough, my dear, why, yes. But wise enough? Who can say?"

The Queen said, "What are you hiding in your hand, my dear, in the folds of your gown?"

The Princess laughed again and said it was a secret.

"Maybe," said the Princess, "it is a flower, or maybe it is a pin for my hair, or maybe it is neither of these; but this very night I will show it you." And again she laughed.

So for the moment they were contented, she was so gay and happy. But when the King and Queen had gone away and were closeted together in their own private room, their fears began to stir in them again, and they decided that the very next day they would tell the Princess of the Fairy Woman and warn her against her wiles.

But, alas! even when the King and the Queen were still talking together, the Princess had taken out the spindle again, and was twisting it in her hand. It was a pretty, slender thing, made cunningly out of the wood of the coral-berried prickwood or spindle-tree, but at one end sharp as a needle. And as she twisted and stayed, twisted and stayed, wondering as she did so why her young fingers were so clumsy, there sounded suddenly in the hush of the evening the wild-yelling screech of an owl at her window. She started, the spindle twisted in her hand, and the sharp point pricked deep into her thumb.

Before even the blood had welled up to the size of a bead upon her thumb, the wicked magic of the Fairy

Woman began to enter into her body. Slowly, drowsily, the Princess's eyelids began to descend over her dark blue eyes; her two hands slid softly down on either side of her; her head drooped lower and lower towards her pillow. She put out her two hands, as if groping her way; sighed; sank lower; and soon she had fallen fast, fast asleep.

Not only the Princess, either. Over the King and Queen, as they sat talking together, a dense, stealthy drowsiness began to descend, though they knew not what had caused it, and they too, in a little while, were mutely slumbering in their chairs. The Lord Treasurer, alone with his money bags, the Astronomer over his charts, the ladies in their chamber, the chief butler in his pantry, and the cooks with their pots and ladles, and the scullions at their basting and boiling, and the maids at their sewing and sweeping—over each and every one of them this irresistible drowsiness descended, and they too were soon asleep.

The grooms in the stables, the gardeners in the garden, the huntsmen and the bee-keepers and the herdsmen and the cowmen and the goat-girl and the goose-girl; the horses feeding at their mangers, the hounds in their kennels, the pigs in their sties, the hawks in their cages, the bees in their skeps, the hens on their roosting-sticks, the birds in the trees and bushes—even the wakeful robin hopping upon the newly-turned clods by the hedgeside, drooped and drowsed; and a deep slumber overwhelmed them one and all.

The fish in the fish-ponds, the flies crawling on the walls, the wasps hovering over the sweetmeats, the moths flitting in search of some old clout in which to lay their eggs, stayed one and all where the magic had found them. All, all were entranced—fell fast, fast asleep.

Throughout the whole castle there was no sound or movement whatsoever, but only the gentle sighings and murmurings of a deep, unfathomable sleep.

Darkness gathered over its battlements and the forests around it; the stars kindled in the sky; and then, at last, the April night gone by, came dawn and daybreak and the returning sun in the east. It glided slowly across the heavens and once more declined into the west; but still all slept on. Days, weeks, months, years went by. Time flowed on, without murmur or ripple, and, wonder of wonders, its passing brought no change.

The Princess, who had been young and lovely, remained young and lovely. The King and Queen aged not at all. They had fallen asleep talking, and the King's bearded mouth was still ajar. The Lord High Chancellor in his gown of velvet, his head at rest upon his money bags, looked not a moment older, though old indeed he looked. A fat scullion standing at a table staring at his fat cheeks and piggy eyes in the bottom of a copper pot continued to stand and stare, and the reflection of those piggy eyes and his tow-coloured mop at the bottom of it changed not at all. The flaxen-haired goose-girl with her switch and her ball of cowslips sat in the meadow as still and young and changeless as her geese. And so it was throughout the castle—the living slumbered on, time flowed away.

But with each returning spring the trees in the garden grew taller and greener, the roses and brambles flung ever wider their hooked and prickled stems and branches. Bindweed and bryony and woodbine and traveller's joy mantled walls and terraces. Wild fruit and bushes of mistletoe flaunted in the orchards. Moss, greener than samphire and seaweed, crept over the stones. The roots of the water-lilies in the moat swelled to the girth of

Asian serpents; its water shallowed; and around the castle there sprang up, and every year grew denser, an immense thorny hedge of white-thorn and briar, which completely encircled it at last with a living wall of green.

At length, nine-and-ninety winters with their ice and snow and darkness had come and gone, and the dense thorn-plaited hedge around the castle began to show the first tiny knobs that would presently break into frail green leaf; the first of spring was come again once more. Wild sang the missel-thrush in the wind and rain. The white-thorn blossomed; the almond-tree; the wilding peach. Then returned the cuckoo, its *cuck-oo* echoing against the castle's walls; and soon the nightingale, sweet in the far thickets.

At last, a little before evening of the last day of April, a Prince from a neighbouring country, having lost his way among mountains that were strange to him in spite of his many wanderings, saw from the hillside the distant turrets of a castle.

Now, when this Prince was a child his nurse had often told him of the sleeping Princess and of the old Fairy Woman's spell, and as he stared down upon the turrets from the hillside the thought came to him that this might be the very castle itself of this old story. So, with his hounds beside him, he came riding down the hill, until he approached and came nearer to the thicket-like hedge that now encircled it even beyond its moat, as if in warning that none should spy or trespass further.

But, unlike other wayfarers who had come and gone, this Prince was not easily turned aside. Having tied his hunting horn to a jutting branch, he made a circuit and rode round the hedge until he came again to the place from which he had started and where his horn was left dangling. But nowhere had he found any break or opening or makeway in the hedge. "Then," thought he, "I must hack my way through." So a little before dark he began to hack his way through with his hunting-knife.

He slashed and slashed at the coarse, prickly branches, pressing on inch by inch until his hands were bleeding and his hunting-gloves in tatters. Darkness came down, and at midnight he hadn't won so much as half-way through the hedge. So he rested himself, made a fire out of the dry twigs and branches, and, exhausted and wearied out, lay down intending to work on by moonlight. Instead, he unwittingly fell fast asleep. But while he slept, a little wind sprang up, and carried a few of the glowing embers of the Prince's fire into the tindery touchwood in the undergrowth of the hedge. There the old, dead leaves began to smoulder, then broke into flame, and by dawn the fire had burnt through the hedge and then stayed. So that when beneath the bright morning sky, wet with dew but refreshed with sleep, the Prince awoke, his way was clear.

He crept through the ashen hole into the garden beyond, full of great trees, many of them burdened with blossom. But there was neither note of bird nor chirp of insect. He made his way over the rotting drawbridge, and went into the castle. And there, as they had fallen asleep a hundred years ago, he saw the King's soldiers and retainers. Outside the guard-house sat two of them, mute as mummies, one with a dice-box between his fingers, for they had been playing with the dice when sleep had come over them a hundred years ago.

At last the Prince came to the bedchamber of the Princess; its door stood ajar, and he looked in. For a while he could see nothing but a green dusk in the room, for its stone windows were overgrown with ivy. He groped slowly nearer to the bed, and looked down upon the sleeper. Her faded silks were worn thin as paper and crumbled like tinder at a touch, yet Time had brought no change at all in her beauty. She lay there in her loveliness, the magic spindle still clasped in her fingers. And the Prince, looking down upon her, had never seen anything in the world so enchanting or so still.

Then, remembering the tale that had been told him, he stooped, crossed himself, and gently kissed the sleeper, then put his hunting-horn to his lips, and sounded a low, but prolonged clear blast upon it, which went echoing on between the stone walls of the castle. It was like the sound of a bugle at daybreak in a camp of soldiers. The Princess sighed; the spindle dropped from her fingers, her lids gently opened, and out of her dark eyes she gazed up into the young man's face. It was as if from being as it were a bud upon its stalk she had become suddenly a flower; and they smiled each at the other.

At this same moment the King, too, stirred, lifted his head, and looked about him, uneasily, as if in search of something. But seeing the dark beloved eyes of the Queen moving beneath their lids, he put out his hand and said, "Ah, my dear!" as if he were satisfied. The Lord High Chancellor, lifting his grey beard from his money table, began to count again his money. The ladies began again to laugh and to chatter over their embroideries. The fat chief butler rose up from stooping over his wine-bottles in the buttery. The cooks began to stir their pots; the scullions began to twist their spits; the grooms began to groom their horses; the gardeners to dig and prune. The huntsmen rode out to their hunting; the cowman drove in his cows; the goat-girl her goats; and the goose-girl in the meadow cried "Ga! ga!" to her geese. There was a neighing of horses and a baying of hounds and a woofing of pigs and a mooing of cows. There was a marvellous shrill crowing of cocks and a singing of birds and a droning of bees and a flitting of butterflies and a buzzing of wasps and a stirring of ants and a cawing of rooks and a murmuration of starlings. The round-eyed robin hopped from clod to clod, and the tiny wren, with cocked-up tail, sang shrill as a bugle amid the walls of the orchards.

For all living things within circuit of the castle at sound of the summons of the Prince's horn had slipped out of their long sleep as easily as a seed of gorse in the hot summer slips out of its pod, or a fish slips from out under a stone. Hearts beat pit-a-pat, tongues wagged, feet clattered, pots clashed, doors slammed, noses sneezed: and soon the whole castle was as busy as a newly-wound clock.

The seventh day afterwards was appointed for the marriage of the Prince and the Princess. But when word was sent far and near, bidding all the Fairy Women to the wedding—and these think no more of time than fish of water—one of them again was absent. And since—early or late—she never came, it seems that come she couldn't. At which the King and Queen heartily rejoiced. The dancing and feasting, with music of harp and pipe and drum and tabor, continued till daybreak; for, after so long a sleep, the night seemed short indeed.

Molly Whuppie

Once upon a time, there was an old woodcutter who had too many children. Work as hard as he might, he couldn't feed them all. So he took the three youngest of them, gave them a last slice of bread and treacle each, and abandoned them in the forest.

They ate the bread and treacle and walked and walked until they were worn out and utterly lost. Soon they would have lain down together like the babes in the wood, and that would have been the end of them if, just as it was beginning to get dark, they had not spied a small and beaming light between the trees. Now this light was chinkling out from a window. So the youngest of them, who was called Molly Whuppie and was by far the cleverest, went and knocked at the door. A woman came to the door and asked them what they wanted. Molly Whuppie said: "Something to eat."

"Eat!" said the woman. "Eat! Why, my husband's a giant, and soon as say knife, he'd eat *you*."

But they were tired out and famished, and still Molly begged the woman to let them in.

So at last the woman took them in, sat them down by the fire on a billet of wood, and gave them some bread and milk. Hardly had they taken a sup of it when there

Mollie Whuppie

came a thumping at the door. No mistaking that: it was the giant come home; and in he came.

"Hai!" he said, squinting at the children. "What have we here?"

"Three poor, cold, hungry, lost little lasses," said his wife. "You get to your supper, my man, and leave them to me."

The giant said nothing, sat down and ate up his supper; but between the bites he looked at the children.

Now the giant had three daughters of his own, and the giant's wife put the whole six of them into the same bed. For so she thought she would keep the strangers safe. But before he went to bed the giant, as if in play, hung three chains of gold round his daughters' necks, and three of golden straw round Molly's and her sisters' between the sheets.

Soon the other five were fast asleep in the great bed, but Molly lay awake listening. At last she rose up softly, and, creeping across, changed over one by one the necklaces of gold and of straw. So now it was Molly and her sisters who wore the chains of gold, and the giant's three daughters the chains of straw. Then she lay down again.

In the middle of the night the giant came tiptoeing into the room, and, groping cautiously with finger and thumb, he plucked up out of the bed the three children with the straw necklaces round their necks, carried them downstairs, and bolted them up in his great cellar.

"So, so, my pretty chickabiddies!" he smiled to himself as he bolted the door, "Now you're safe!"

As soon as all was quiet again, Molly Whuppie thought it high time she and her sisters were out of that house. So she woke them, whispering in their ears, and they slipped down the stairs together and out into the forest, and never stopped running till morning.

But daybreak came at last, and lo and behold, they came to another house. It stood beside a pool of water full of wild swans, and stone images there, and a thousand windows; and it was the house of the King. So Molly went in, and told her story to the King. The King listened, and when it was finished, said:

"Well, Molly, that's one thing done, and done well. But I could tell another thing, and that would be a better." This King, indeed, knew the giant of old; and he told Molly that if she would go back and steal for him the giant's sword that hung behind his bed, he would give her eldest sister his eldest son for a husband, and then Molly's sister would be a princess.

Molly looked at the eldest prince, for there they all sat at breakfast, and she smiled and said she would try.

So, that very evening, she muffled herself up, and made her way back through the forest to the house of the giant. First she listened at the window, and there she heard the giant eating his supper; so she crept into the house and hid herself under his bed.

In the middle of the night—and the shutters fairly shook with the giant's snoring—Molly climbed softly up on to the great bed and unhooked the giant's sword that was dangling from its nail in the wall. Lucky it was for Molly this was not the giant's great fighting sword, but only a little sword. It was heavy enough for all that, and when she came to the door, it rattled in its scabbard and woke up the giant.

Then Molly ran, and the giant ran, and they both ran, and at last they came to the Bridge of the One Hair, and Molly ran over. But not the giant; for run over he couldn't. Instead, he shook his fist at her across the great chasm in between, and shouted:

*"Woe betide ye, Molly Whuppie,
If ye e'er come back again!"*

But Molly only laughed and said:

*"Maybe twice I'll come to see 'ee,
If so be I come to Spain."*

Then Molly carried off the sword to the King; and her eldest sister married the King's eldest son.

"Well," said the King, when the wedding was over, "that was a better thing done, Molly, and done well. But I know another, and that's better still. Steal the purse that lies under the giant's pillow, and I'll marry your second sister to my second son."

Molly looked at the King's second son, and laughed, and said she would try.

So she muffled herself up in another-coloured hood, and stole off through the forest to the giant's house, and there he was, guzzling as usual at supper. This time she hid herself in his linen closet. A stuffy place that was.

About the middle of the night, she crept out of the linen closet, took a deep breath, and pushed in her fingers just a little bit betwixt his bolster and pillow. The giant stopped snoring and sighed, but soon began to snore again. Then Molly slid her fingers in a little bit further under his pillow. At this the giant called out in his sleep as if there were robbers near. And his wife said: "Lie easy, man! It's those bones you had for supper."

Then Molly pushed in her fingers even a little bit further, and then they felt the purse. But as she drew out the purse from under the pillow, a gold piece dropped out of it and clanked on to the floor, and at sound of it the giant woke.

Then Molly ran, and the giant ran, and they both ran. And they both ran and ran until they came to the Bridge of the One Hair. And Molly got over, but the giant stayed; for get over he couldn't. Then he cried out on her across the chasm:

> "*Woe betide ye, Molly Whuppie,*
> *If ye e'er come back again!*"

But Molly only laughed, and called back at him:

> "*Once again I'll come to see 'ee,*
> *If so be I come to Spain.*"

So she took the purse to the King, and her second sister married his second son; and there were great rejoicings.

"Well, well," said the King to Molly, when the feasting was over, "that was yet a better thing done, Molly, and done for good. But I know a better yet, and that's the best of all. Steal the giant's ring for me from off his thumb, and you shall have my youngest son for yourself. And all solemn, Molly, you always were my favourite."

Molly laughed and looked at the King's youngest son, turned her head, frowned, then laughed again, and said she would try. This time, when she had stolen into the giant's house, she hid in the chimney niche.

At dead of night, when the giant was snoring, she stepped out of the chimney niche and crept towards the bed. By good chance the giant lay on his back, his head on his pillow, with his arm hanging down out over the bedside, and it was the arm that had the hand at the end of it on which was the great thumb that wore the ring. First Molly wetted the giant's thumb, then she tugged softly and softly at the ring. Little by little it slid down and down over the knuckle-bone; but just as Molly had slipped it off and pushed it into her pocket, the giant woke with a roar, clutched at her, gripped her, and lifted her clean up into the dark over his head.

"Ah-ha! Molly Whuppie!" says he. "Once too many is never again. Ay, and if *I'd* done the ill to you as the ill you have done's been done to me, what would I be getting for *my* pains?"

"Why," says Molly all in one breath, "I'd bundle you up into a sack, and I'd put the cat and dog inside with you, and a needle and thread and a great pair of shears, and I'd hang you up on the wall, be off to the wood, cut the thickest stick I could get, come home, take you down, and beat you to a jelly. *That's* what I'd do!"

"And that, Molly," says the giant, chuckling to himself with pleasure and pride at his cunning, "that's just what I will be doing with you." So he rose up out of his bed and fetched a sack, put Molly into the sack, and the cat and the dog besides, and a needle and thread and a stout pair of shears, and hung her up on the wall. Then away he went into the forest to cut a cudgel.

When he was well gone, Molly, stroking the dog with one hand and the cat with the other, sang out in a high, clear, jubilant voice: "Oh, if only everybody could see what I can see!"

" 'See,' Molly?" said the giant's wife. "What do you see?"

But Molly only said, "Oh, if only everybody could see what I see! Oh, if only they could see what *I* see!"

At last the giant's wife begged and entreated Molly to take her up into the sack so that she could see what Molly saw. Then Molly took the shears and cut a hole in the lowest corner of the sack, jumped out of the sack, helped the giant's wife up into it, and, as fast as she could, sewed up the hole with the needle and thread.

But it was pitch black in the sack, so the giant's wife saw nothing but stars, and they were inside of her, and she soon began to ask to be let out again. Molly never heeded or answered her, but hid herself far in at the back of the door. Home at last came the giant, with a quick-wood cudgel in his hand and a knob on the end of it as big as a pumpkin. And he began to belabour the sack with the cudgel.

His wife cried: "Stay, man! It's me, man! Oh, man, it's me, man!" But the dog barked and the cat squalled, and at first he didn't hear her voice.

Then Molly crept softly out from behind the door. But the giant saw her. He gave a roar. And Molly ran, and the giant ran, and they both ran, and they ran and they ran and they ran—Molly and the giant—till they came to the Bridge of the One Hair. And Molly skipped along over it; but the giant stayed, for he couldn't. And he cried out after her in a dreadful voice across the chasm:

" *Woe betide ye, Molly Whuppie,*
   If ye e'er come back again!"

But Molly waved her hand at the giant over the chasm,
and flung back her head:

" Never *again I'll come to see 'ee,*
   Though so be I come to Spain."

Then Molly ran off with the ring in her pocket, and
she was married to the King's youngest son; and there
was a feast that was a finer feast than all the feasts that had
ever been in the King's house before, and there were
lights in all the windows.

Lights so bright that all the dark long the hosts of the
wild swans swept circling in space under the stars. But
though there were guests by the hundred from all parts
of the country, the giant never so much as gnawed a bone!

Rapunzel

———————◦›❈‹◦———————

In a cottage near the garden of an old woman who knew magic and was a sorceress there was a small square window under the thatch of the roof, and at this window the woman who lived in the cottage delighted to sit and look out. There were strange and far-fetched flowers and herbs and plants in the garden of the sorceress, and the air was full of their sweet smells; but the one thing she wanted most as she sat at her window gazing over the wall was some rampions.

There they were in plenty, blooming freely in the garden, with their pale blue clusters of bell-like flowers. But it was not these this woman longed for and pined after most, but the sweet roots of the rampions for a salad. That evening she told her husband, who was a wood-cutter, that she must have some, or die. "A dish or even so much as a taste of those rampions," she entreated him, "or I die!"

At last, though he was full of fear of the sorceress, he climbed over the wall, and plucked up some of the roots. But the sorceress, when she went walking in her garden that evening, spying this way and that, knew that some of her rampions had been stolen, and she watched. The next time the woodcutter set out to climb over the wall —for his wife gave him no peace—the sorceress spied

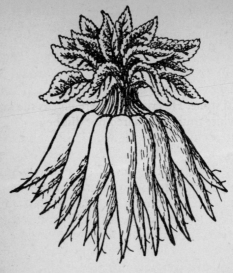

him out through the trees. And she called out to him in a
strange tongue, and he could move neither hand nor foot.

So he must needs tell the sorceress why he had come;
and in his fear, he promised to do whatever the old
woman asked him. She let him go free only on one
condition—that, if ever they had one, he and his wife
would promise to give up their first child to her.

Now, a little while after this a baby was born which
the woodcutter and his wife called Rapunzel, for it means
rampion or bell-flower. In fear of the sorceress they hid
the baby for some little time, but at last the poor woman
died, and when one day the woodcutter was away in the
forest at his work, Rapunzel got up on to a stool and
looked out of the little window under the roof, and for
the first time peeped into the old sorceress's garden. It
was fresh with the dew of morning, and green and fair in
the sunshine.

She gazed into it with delight, and drank in its sweetness. But, alas! the sorceress espied her at the window, and when the woodcutter came home she was awaiting him, and threatened that if he did not keep the vow he had made and let Rapunzel go, she would with her enchantments turn the child into a toad, and himself into a lump of stone. He cringed before her, as she sat on high on her white mule, and dared not disobey.

With tears in his eyes the woodcutter kissed Rapunzel for the last time, stroked her hair, and bade her goodbye. And the sorceress, seeing how lovely the child was, with her fair skin and golden hair, took her away into the forest and shut her up in a small chamber at the top of a stone tower. There, every evening, the sorceress used to visit her; and because she was afraid if, whenever she came, she opened the door of the tower with her key she might some day lose the key, she mused within herself and thought of another way by which she could climb up to Rapunzel's room in the tower.

This was her way. When the sorceress in the evening twilight called under the tower, "I come, Rapunzel," the child would let down her long gold hair, having already wound its plaits twice round a bar in the window. Then the old woman would climb up as if by a ladder, and so into her room. But Rapunzel feared and hated the sorceress, and dreaded her coming. She pined to escape and flee away from her enchantments. But for years she pined in vain.

Now one summer's day the King's youngest son was riding in the forest, and having missed his way, approached by chance the tower of the sorceress, and heard a singing, but not of birds. Indeed, it was the voice of Rapunzel, who was now seventeen, and so well used to being alone that she hardly knew how lonely she was or

how much she yearned for company. She sat in solitude
at her window in the tower and was singing softly over
her needle:

> *"Ah-la-la, ah, la-la,*
> *And O la, a-la-la . . ."*

The Prince listened to this wordless song, and the sound
of it was beyond comparison sweet and clear, stealing
his very thoughts away.

Even when the singing was ended he remained silent
under the trees, for the notes sounded on in his mind as if
—like the sea-nymphs'—they were the echo of a voice
heard long ago. He kept watch, and a little while after he
saw the old sorceress come riding in on her mule, and
draw rein beneath the window; and heard her say: "I
come, Rapunzel!" Then in amazement he watched the
sorceress mount up to Rapunzel's window by the ladder
of gold hair.

The next day the Prince towards evening, but an hour
earlier, came to the tower, and himself stood at its foot
under the window and called softly, and in a voice unlike
his own: "I come, Rapunzel!"

When, instead of the face of the sorceress, the face of
the young Prince showed at the window, Rapunzel at
first could not speak for fear and astonishment. But the
Prince comforted her, and was gentle, and said that all
his hope was only to help her. The next day he came again
to see Rapunzel, and then again. At last her one thought
was of him. Her eyes were now clear as sunbeams in
winter, she sang half the day through, pining for evening,
and in spite of her solitude she always had company.
Then, at last, one day the Prince persuaded Rapunzel to
try to win away the key of the tower from the old
sorceress.

"Then," said he, "you can let yourself out of the door at the foot of the tower, and I will carry you away in safety to my mother, the Queen, who will love you dearly."

But when he had left Rapunzel, he felt, though he knew not why, ill at ease, and instead of riding away at once he stayed and lingered near the tower, though out of sight of it, and waited and watched.

Yet again, and early in the evening, the sorceress came to the tower, and climbed up to Rapunzel. They sat together, and the last blood-red of the sun was in the west. And Rapunzel, as she sat bent over her sewing, her face bowed down, asked the old sorceress if she might have the key of the tower. "Then I could myself let you in whenever you come," she said, "and it would spare your breath."

"And what tongue in a dream," said the sorceress, "put *that* into your head?" She looked at Rapunzel, her eyes cold and still as a serpent's.

And Rapunzel, still stooping over her sewing, and without thinking, replied: "You take such a long, long time to climb up."

"Ah!" cried the sorceress in a rage, "and how did you learn *that*, wicked deceiver, unless some meddling stranger has climbed up to tell you it? Hearken to me, Rapunzel: prince or no prince, he that comes to spy shall have his eyes put out. Ay, and his tongue too. As for you, be ready for me at daybreak to-morrow, and with my bright sharp scissors we will trim a few strands of that fine gold hair." Trembling with anger, she climbed down again out of the window, and rode away to her own mansion in the green garden, on her mule.

But the Prince, keeping watch in the forest, had heard her shrill voice as she talked to Rapunzel, and as soon as she was safely gone he came stealthily to the tower and called: "I come, Rapunzel!" And by her hair he climbed up yet again to her window.

The first stars were glowing in the sky, and it was dark night over the forest. Rapunzel was weeping. She told him of the evil designs of the sorceress, and entreated him to be gone and to come again no more. But the Prince comforted her. They talked together in voices so low and secret that even the crickets' shrilled loud above them, and in a while they agreed what should be done on the morrow. And the Prince gave Rapunzel his hunting-knife.

At daybreak next morning the sorceress came again to the tower, with her lean-bladed scissors, and worse besides. The sun was not yet risen, and mist like milk lay over the glades of the forest, but the birds in the woods were beginning to waken, and the sorceress cried: "I come, Rapunzel."

And she climbed, and she climbed, and she climbed up the golden ladder of Rapunzel's hair until she was almost within touch of the window. Then, but not till then, with the Prince's hunting-knife in her hand, Rapunzel began to saw and saw at the plaits of her own hair, until at last she cut through every strand, and the old sorceress fell from the tower flat to the ground. And the scissors she carried pierced clean through to her heart. So her evil was over.

Then the Prince took the key of the tower out of its leather wallet in the mule's red saddle, and himself mounted up the stairs. Soon he and Rapunzel were galloping off together through the forest. Merrily rang his riding bells and merrily rang their voices, while Rapunzel's hair flowed down and away from his saddle-bow as if it were a stream of sunbeams made solid as gold.